BLOOD & TACOS
presents

BATTLEGROUND U.S.S.A.:
RED DUSK

A NOVEL BY
MAX AUGER

discovered by **CHRISTOPHER BLAIR**

SOVIET
ALASKA

VICHY CANADA

FREE

UNITED
SOCIALIST
STATES OF
AMERICA

U

UNOCCUPIED
LOS ANGELES

DEMOCRATIC PEOPLE'S
REPUBLIC OF MEXICO

DETAIL OF BERING STRAIT

Чукотское
море

полуостров
Сибиряк

лагерь
Жуков
D

Советская
Армия
трехлотуг

CAPTURED PLANS

SINO-HAWAIIAN ANNEXATION

北

阿罗哈同志
夏威夷省

C A N A D A

S. A.

KEY

BATTLE FRONT

NUCLEAR STRIKES

CUBAN
FLORIDA

SOVIET JAMAICA

First Printing, 2015
ISBN 978-1-926946-00-9

Creative Guy Publishing
Victoria, Canada

BATTLEGROUND U.S.S.A.: RED DUSK

PROLOGUE: PART ONE

A Mikoyan MiG-31R
67,000 feet over Colorado

The pilot was drunk.

From the MiG's rear seat, Lieutenant Oleg Kokorin tried to monitor the plane's instruments with one eye and the back of Colonel Fyodorov's helmet with the other. Fyodorov's head had bobbed and jerked awake for the past hour, bright white against the black sky of the stratosphere. Flying backseat with a man like Fyodorov, even on a boring, high-and-fast reconnaissance mission like this one, should have been an honor. But young Kokorin and the rest of the air force knew everything about the big, grizzled Ukrainian up front. Knew of his record over Vietnam and America. Kokorin also knew that Fyodorov liked his drink. With his beloved vodka hard to come by at the Mexican bases, the old man had adapted to the barbaric tequila. Fyodorov had reeked of the stuff back at the fighter base in Hermosillo. That morning, the legendary ace had ignored Kokorin's crisp salute and wobbled up the ladder into the cockpit.

A half hour later, over the American West, the young lieutenant tried to keep his fears at bay. They were flying the fastest plane of the entire war—scraping the edge of space at Mach 2.7. If Fyodorov could dry out and fly straight and true, they might evade detection by the Americans far below.

For his first and hopefully only flight with Fyodorov, Kokorin knew he had a job to do. He just did not know what it was. The equipment was ready. He could not bear it any longer. "Permit me to say that it is an honor to fly with you today, Comrade Colonel!" Kokorin saw the edge of the pilot's helmet jerk at the sound of his voice, then sink again. Over the intercom, Kokorin heard the unmistakable sound of a choked, drunken snore.

He cleared his throat. "Comrade Colonel!"

A moment later, he heard the old pilot's voice: "Lieutenant Kokorin, please spare me the courtesies. You are safe with me. The KGB and all interested parties are doing their work on the ground far below us."

"Yes, Comrade Colonel, I suppose that this is true."

Fyodorov raised a gloved hand. "Take in the view, my boy!" he said. "To the left, our conquered territory of western America. Below us, the broad spine of the Rocky Mountains, and our brave warriors. To our right, the Great Plains—and the glory to come!"

"Yes, Comrade Colonel, it is a good day to fly," Kokorin said. "And now, at the risk of sounding abrupt, we are almost in position. My orders require me to verify…"

The colonel had been chuckling halfway through Kokorin's request. It grew into a hearty laugh. "Lieutenant Kokorin," Fyodorov said. "Your eagerness inspires this old servant of the working class. The time has come to initiate Reconnaissance Plan Alpha." The colonel then mumbled a sequence of numbers and letters. Kokorin entered them into the MiG-31's computer. The readouts told Kokorin that the cameras had begun working in the compartment below him. He leaned forward into the monitoring scope, and saw a dimmer view of what the cameras collected in sharper detail.

"We are gathering data, Comrade Colonel!"

"Good, Lieutenant, good! When we have delivered your images to GRU in Alaska, I will fly you down to Acapulco. You will spend the rest of the war with a beautiful Mexican girl on each arm!"

Distasteful. "Thank you… but I am engaged to be married, Comrade Colonel!"

From the front seat, the colonel laughed, long and sorrowful. "Oh, dear Lieutenant Kokorin, you have my deepest sympathies."

Kokorin found himself thinking of his sweet Natalya. The year apart from her had been hell. Focusing on his mission would be best. "Our cameras are imaging Colorado Springs," he reported. It would have been more accurate to say what was *left* of Colorado Springs. On the first day of the war, R-36M missiles had hit the city and its surrounding military installations thirty-five times. The city, the mountain base of NORAD, Fort Carson, Peterson Air Force Base, even the Americans' air force school—all of it now a black sunburst twenty miles wide on the dead and dying Colorado plains.

"Lieutenant Kokorin, what is that infernal whining that I hear?" the colonel asked.

Kokorin checked the scope. "That is lingering radiation from last year's missile strikes," he replied. "We are not in danger. It is affecting our more sensitive equipment, but nothing that will stop us in our mission."

"Do you see any evidence of troop movements or equipment?"

Kokorin peered through the scope. "I see a highway to the north. Crowded. Vehicles. Refugees, perhaps."

The colonel chuckled. "No, no, Lieutenant Kokorin. The first phase of our mission is complete. That is what remains of the Americans' fabled First Armored Division, rushing to engage our men in the mountains. Continue to monitor the cameras until I give the signal. Then, on to Soviet Alaska, yes?"

"Yes, Comrade Colonel." Kokorin leaned back in his seat and breathed from his mask. The minutes dragged, each one putting them fifty precious kilometers closer to Alaska. If there were a God above their canopy, any moment now, Fyodorov would bank the MiG-31 to the northwest. They would refuel over Yellowstone, then they fly toward the Pacific.

But not if the old man, in his drunken incompetence, tried to kill them first: "Colonel, our airspeed!" Kokorin cried. "We are at two thousand and dropping! Our altitude—we have descended below fifteen thousand meters!"

"Lieutenant Kokorin, I do not see the same result," Fyodorov slurred. But to his credit, the old man sounded serious. For once! "Could the Americans be jamming our instruments from the ground?"

"I am not sure if such a thing is—wait! We are detected! Would it please the Colonel to increase our altitude and speed?"

"Steady, Lieutenant. I will fly the aircraft."

"Comrade Colonel! I have two SAM launches on my scope! Patriot missiles! Nineteen kilometers and closing!" *No! The worst was happening!* "They have launched again! Now a third launch! Prepare to deploy countermeasures!"

But Kokorin knew it was too late. The alarms already

shrieked in his ear, three different tones for the three missiles arcing toward them at five times the speed of sound. The old man was gunning the throttle and pulling them into a climb, but this would just make the Patriots' job easier. The Lieutenant reached for the ejection handle as a miniature sun flared just to his right and blasted away the MiG's right wing. A split second later, the second Patriot flew into the plane's right exhaust and exploded.

The blast threw Kokorin forward into his instrument panel in a shower of glass and sparks. His collarbones snapped against the heavy straps holding him in place. By now, the plane was already smoking wreckage, spinning toward the earth.

Less than a minute later, just as he slammed into the Colorado high plains, Lieutenant Kokorin's last thoughts were of his beloved Natalya—and the worthless Ukrainian, the drunkard, in the front seat.

PROLOGUE: PART TWO

Aug. 2, 1989
Royal Gorge Bridge
Cañon City, Colorado

Descending beneath his MC1-1C special forces parachute, Mike McCreary felt the crunch of the Soviet private's cervical vertebrae travel from the soles of his boots all the way up into his war-weary heart. An instant after striking the soldier's neck, McCreary pulled his parachute's toggles and braked to a graceful stop atop the collapsing corpse. The black canopy deflated and covered both hunter and prey. McCreary crouched over the twitching body. He waited for the man's comrades to open fire.

Nothing happened. No one had seen his chute, or those of the seven others behind him. Impossible—the Russian platoon had sent a single man to patrol the single-lane bridge's entire quarter-mile span while the rest smoke and drank at either end. Communist incompetence or dumb luck?

Seconds after he and his men had started their High Altitude/Low Open jump, their C-130 had erupted in flame from a max-range R-73 Vympel air-to-air strike.

9

The second bit of bad news had arrived halfway through their free-fall: their evac chopper had been hit, too. Now, even if they sent the bridge to the bottom of the Royal Gorge ahead of the oncoming Soviet division, they faced a 20-mile hike to the American lines.

Since the invasion, McCreary had learned a thing or two about luck. It was a yo-yo, up one second, down the next. By hitting the Hercules and the Black Hawk, the Russians showed that they knew something was amiss. But they hadn't bothered to tell the soldiers at the bridge. When a heart-stopping thirty seconds had passed, McCreary crawled out from under the canopy. He looked to either end of the span. A line of ghostly yellow lanterns cast a chain of faint ovals, separated by inky shadow. In the distance, out of sight, McCreary could hear Russians muttering, occasionally laughing. He stood and detached his canopy. Wrapping the dead sentry in it took thirty seconds, way longer than he wanted. McCreary dragged the dead private to the railing and sent it over the side. The Arkansas River was more than a thousand feet below. When the Russian hit the water—or the rocks—McCreary never heard it.

He invaded my home, McCreary tried to tell himself. *Let him fall all the way to hell.*

Time for Phase 2. McCreary silently hit the deck and extended the bipod of his M21 sniper rifle. Just then, Private Billy LaRoy landed next to him with a soft thud. The West Virginian had his canopy off and balled up in seconds. LaRoy lay beside McCreary, facing the other direction, already peering through his own M21's scope.

LaRoy whispered, "They were right behind me, sir. What's keepin' 'em?"

As if in answer to McCreary's silent prayer, the demo team arrived, three on either side of them, landing within four or five seconds of one another. With little acknowledgement to McCreary and LaRoy, they went to work.

The plan called for forty kilos of C-4, some of it lashed to the cables, but most cut into the support towers with the sappers' smokeless acetylene torches. Watching the men work, McCreary marveled at the training of the Army's finest specialists. These men were phantoms. The fact that the good guys were losing this war was a crying shame.

When it was over, who would mourn the greatest country the world had ever known?

Within minutes, the operation was all over but the shouting. McCreary, LaRoy, and the sappers faded back to the east end of the bridge. The 163rd Motor Rifles' Division approached from the west to cut off Interstate 25. Lieutenant Dan Dunsuir hunkered down next to McCreary. His boots glinted dully in the starlight, pure West Point. "Just about done, sir," he said. "Say the word, and we'll move on to that command post on the east end."

"How far up the road is that Russian column?" McCreary whispered.

Without checking his watch, Dunsmuir said, "Three minutes. The good news is, this is the last goddamn bridge in the state."

"And if we don't blow this one," McCreary said, "it's all they'll need."

McCreary disappeared into the green-hued world offered by his Starlight scope. Just past the darting phantom demolition men, McCreary counted eight Russian silhouettes, mostly upper torsos, none of them facing the bridge. They'd miss their single sentry soon.

The Starlight scope went grainy. Something farther out was washing the picture. McCreary spotted dancing headlights, far in the distance. It was time to go. There'd be no time for a fancy, choreographed exit.

It was time to go.

Now.

McCreary turned and hissed at LaRoy: "Ivan's comin'. Hit the command post. I'll cover you. Give the signal, I'll blow the bridge."

LaRoy already was shaking his head. "No, sirree, Captain. We ain't gonna get separated again."

Back to Dunsmuir: "Gimme the switch, Lieutenant. You have a long hike back ahead of you."

The young, fair-haired lieutenant refused: "I've got orders, Captain. General Pearce said you'd try something like this. He said you're too valuable to—"

A distant growl arose, one of tanks and diesel engines. McCreary leaned in. "You got kids, son," he muttered, "and we ain't got time. Hand it over. That contraption can't have a range of more than a hundred feet."

Dunsmuir hesitated and shook his head in defeat. He pulled the wireless detonator out of his front pouch, placed it in McCreary's left hand with both of his. He twisted the bottom. The device blinked once, red, in McCreary's fist. "I guess that's it for my ass," Dunsmuir sighed, gingerly letting go. "I'll tell the old man that you're up to your old tricks. Good thing we still have control of Leavenworth, right?"

"I wouldn't worry about prison," McCreary said, tightening his grip on the detonator. "You boys are the only demolition team left in the entire U.S. Army. Now *git*. And give the general my regards."

McCreary turned back to his scope. He'd learned long ago that sometimes all a man had to do to win an argument was turn his head.

He felt LaRoy's heavy hand thump his back. "Good luck, sir. I'll see you back at the ranch." Then the fading sounds of running boot heels told McCreary all he needed to know. He was alone, ready to stop the advancing elements of an entire Soviet tank division by blowing the highest suspension bridge in the world—and probably ride the entire thing down. Until then, every Red he bagged would be one fewer for America to deal with.

In the dark behind him, Dunsmuir, LaRoy, and the rest were already at work. McCreary heard the muffled thumps of silenced semi-automatic rifle fire. It went on for a few seconds before the unit scored its first messy kill: a Communist scream cut the night before being drowned out by another hail of bullets.

The scream got the attention of the soldiers on the bridge's west end. Through his scope, McCreary saw a flurry of activity as Russians tossed their cigarettes and made furtive grabs for their weapons. With one hand clutching the detonator and the other arm cradling his M21, McCreary squeezed the trigger. The Soviets jerked and twisted like dark marionettes. Skulls burst under a well-aimed volley of 7.62x51mm ammunition. McCreary ejected his empty clip and reloaded. He stood as the lead jeep from the 163rd drove onto the bridge. It was a UAZ-469. McCreary couldn't make out the driver's face, which made it easy to shatter the windshield. With its driver's foot still on the gas, it lurched forward and drove its front tires over the bridge's railing, where they hung, spinning.

Behind him, an explosion from the command center almost pushed McCreary forward onto his face. He turned, and saw a bright orange fireball boiling above him, turning night into day.

"Good work, boys," he muttered. McCreary turned and advanced on the jeep. An officer burst out of the back, brandishing an automatic in each hand; McCreary hit him with three rounds in the chest. Behind the jeep, a GAZ-66 truck charged onto the bridge. It clipped the UAZ and sent it tumbling over the side, then bounced over the officer's body. Still a hundred yards away, McCreary heard the heavy throb of king-sized Soviet diesel engine. Headlights grew brighter by the second.

Holding the detonator and stepping backward, McCreary opened fire from his waist. He put six rounds into the windshield. The glass turned gray but didn't break. Then the truck was on him. McCreary thought about blowing the bridge, but something made him turn to run. Maybe it was the thought of seeing Sunny again.

To the sound of squealing brakes, McCreary turned around into a half dozen AK-47 barrels, silhouetted by the flames from the command center. The men pointing them at his head were scorched, bloodied, angry—and alive.

So this was the end. He might as well go out shooting. *Click.*

He'd forgotten to eject his clip and reload. Did he even have any rounds left? Why had he gotten so sloppy lately? Did he even want to live at all?

Good question.

A horde of soldiers poured out of the GAZ and surrounded him. A doughy-faced, unshaved Russian sergeant yelled commands at the command post survivors. One of them turned and gestured toward the dark horizon. McCreary could tell that he was making excuses; LaRoy and the others had gotten away. McCreary smiled. He dropped his rifle and slowly backed away toward the railing.

The sergeant gestured toward the flaming visitor's center, and yelled questions at McCreary in Russian. The command post? Who cared? It was then that McCreary realized a little bit of good fortune: *they don't know we're blowing the bridge at all*. McCreary lowered his left hand. "Say," he asked, "any of you boys speak American?"

For a moment, there was silence. Then:

"Yes, Yankee."

A young man of low rank stepped in front of the other men. "I speak English," he said. Unlike the crew he was running with, the private was a good-looking kid. He looked all of eighteen. Blond. Blue eyed. A little like Sunny. By now, a long line of trucks, APC's and jeeps had pulled onto the bridge, engines idling. Soldiers piled out. If this bridge weren't built to handle five hundred tons of Russian steel, they'd all find out soon enough.

"Do not be sad, Yankee," the blond private said. "Yes, you will die tonight. But know that we love America, too! We have come for your apple pie! Your pretty American girls! Your Levis 501s!"

McCreary smiled and shook his head. "What's your name, son?" he asked.

The kid laughed again. He released the barrel of his AK-47 and pointed at his chest. "Me? What is *my* name?"

McCreary nodded and smiled: "That's right."

The Russian looked left and right at his squad, laughing. *Get a load of this guy.* The platoon joined in. It was a regular stand-up comedy show, and McCreary was the opening act. The Russian private shrugged, all smiles. "Okay, I am Yuri! Hello! How-dee-doo, eh? And what is your name, Yankee?"

"I'm Captain Mike McCreary, United States Air Force."

The kid's eyebrows went up in surprise. *"Oh! USA Air Force! USA Kapitan!"* He stood a little straighter, thumped his boot heels, and saluted McCreary as though he were addressing Stalin himself. McCreary returned the salute. As he did, the kid turned to his buddies and laughed again.

"Come, Yankee," Yuri said. "KGB is on their way. They are biggest fan!" He gestured with his rifle toward the west end of the bridge.

McCreary rubbed his jaw, and shook his head. "Well, I'd love to, Yuri, but see, it's like this: I've wired this bridge with enough C-4 to blow you and all your friends back to Leningrad."

The kid's smile faded. The rest of the patrol sensed Yuri's sudden discomfort but didn't understand. They looked to the back of the kid's head for clues. "You know?" McCreary said to the entire group, helpfully. "C-4? *Kaboom!*" The Russians knew "kaboom." They flinched. A few backed away toward the truck.

One reached the railing. He peered over the side and spotted something he didn't like. *"Vzryvchatyye veshchestva! On provodnoy ves' most! My trakhal!"*

McCreary raised his right arm. He raised his voice: "You boys see this little thingamobber, here?"

Yuri raised his AK-47 in a much more menacing posture. "Let it drop!" he commanded.

"Now, see, Yuri, that'd be a mistake." McCreary gestured at the device. "This here's what we call a dead man's switch. You shoot me, I let go, and this bridge'll take a tumble. All the way down."

Somewhere in the darkness, McCreary heard the faint cry of an eagle.

He made a halting thrust with his arm. Every Russian soldier flinched. McCreary smiled. The soldiers walked backward, gingerly, as though their footsteps might set off the whole thing. But to Yuri's credit, the kid stayed put. His was the only AK still aimed in McCreary's direction. "You boys skedaddle, now!" McCreary called. Apparently, the other men knew *skedaddle.* The platoon scurried and pushed past each other to get off the bridge. A minute passed, then two. Most of the outfit had cleared the bridge, and didn't stop until they reached the other side.

That left McCreary and his new friend, Yuri. The barrel of his AK-47 remained pointed at McCreary's forehead. The kid was going to try and win the war all by himself.

McCreary turned his back on the kid and stepped toward the railing. He wondered what the kid might do—shoot him in the back? rush him and hope for the best?—then realized that he didn't care. McCreary peered down at the river. Tingles went up and down the backs of his thighs. A thousand feet over the railing, he could see the Arkansas River snaking ghostly white through jagged boulders.

"You know, Yuri," he said, "I been fightin' this war more'n a year now." He rubbed the railing with his free hand. Slow. Thoughtful. "And I'm tired of it. Real tired." McCreary closed his eyes and raised his foot.

"McCreary!" he heard Yuri cry. *"What are you doing?"*

With dizzying speed, McCreary pushed himself up the railing and turned back around. He wobbled a bit but caught his balance. A stiff breeze would knock him into oblivion.

"Come down off railing!" Yuri yelled. *"I will shoot you!"*

McCreary kept on: "See, one of your Soviet generals a while back, he came a-callin' on my hometown. He did a real number on my wife. Brainwashed her. He made it so she ... she don't think she's American no more.

She speaks Russian. *Acts* Russian. Maybe even *thinks* in Russian, for all I know."

McCreary took a deep breath and lifted his face to the sky. He could see Sunny in the Milky Way. Her smile. Her mischievous eyes. "I tell you what, Yuri," he said, his voice far away, "You boys are over here doin' a job. Someone older and dumber'n you's makin' you do it. This ain't nothin' personal. It's been a fair fight up to now. But I'll tell you what—you mess with a man's woman, you give him nothin' left to live for."

If there were any thought of running in the kid's eyes, McCreary couldn't see it. The young soldier was motivated. The Russian smiled, but his eyes turned to steel.

"We know what General Azov did to wife, Yankee," he said. "Every Russian soldier knows about wife of *Kapitan* Mike McCreary. When we are lonely and miss our home, we tell stories about your Sunny. Because someday, Yankee… we all will have an American wife of our own." Yuri began to laugh again.

"Goodbye, Yuri," McCreary said quietly. And sprung backward into the warm evening air.

"NYET!!! NYET!!! NYET!!!"

Falling, his face aimed up at the breeze, McCreary saw wild orange tracers cut the dark above his head. Yuri had fired too late. As the kid's face appeared over the railing, McCreary simultaneously let go of the switch and pulled the cord on his reserve chute.

A series of fireballs gripped and twisted the bridge like a row of orange fists. McCreary spun in the air like a leaf. He caught mad, swirling glimpses of the canyon walls. He sailed away from the collapsing bridge, but mostly fell. Above him, the small emergency chute half inflated, collapsed, and inflated again. Finally, as the entire structure of the bridge groaned hellishly, flaming, into the gorge a dozen yards to his right, the chute caught a scoop of air. McCreary made two swings before he landed hard on a soft, gravelly beach. He rolled several times, tangled in his shroud. Something exploded behind him in the wreckage of the bridge. McCreary, so damned tired of this war, didn't even flinch.

"I made it," he said aloud, as if to prove it to himself. "I'm alive. Damn shame."

McCreary stood and released his chute, and for a full minute he watched it spin and tumble into the dark like a ghost.

When it was gone, McCreary scrambled over the rocks and twisted metal wreckage, upriver, into darkness.

DAY ONE

Sept. 21, 1989
Forward Command Base Alpha
First Infantry Division
Cheyenne, Wyo.

"Look at this, Sunny: Your husband just won the Medal of Honor!"

From her little bunk in the corner of her cage, the woman that McCreary had known as Sunny narrowed her eyes at him.

McCreary pointed at the ring around his finger and pointed at her. He nodded, encouraging her, trying to forget that she had hurled her own ring at him right after her rescue. Now, in her plain but clean blue peasant's dress, she ignored his bright, almost childlike smile—and spat toward the bars that surrounded her.

"Gryaznaya amerikanskaya svin'ya!" she hissed. *"Ya zhena Generala Yuriya Azov, Sovetskoy Armya! Skazhi mne, chto ty sdelals moim muzhem!"*

With a shaky hand, McCreary pulled a chair away from his makeshift desk. He spun it around and sat on it backward, facing his wife's ten-by-ten cage. His lanky, powerful arms draped over the seatback, McCreary struggled to hold onto his smile.

The young translator standing behind him asked, "Want me to tell you want she said, Major?"

McCreary sighed and shook his head. He looked at his wife. Through the bars, past her hate. That honey-colored hair. Such a pretty girl. Without looking at the medal around his neck, he ran his fingers over its five points.

Sunny unleashed another barrage of pure Russian hate at McCreary. He ignored her and tried to keep talking, the way the base shrink had urged him to. "Speak English, sweetheart," McCreary said. "My God! What'd that bastard do to you?"

"Vy mne kletku kak svin'ya. No tysvin'ya!"

McCreary pinched the bridge of his nose. "All right, what did she say?"

The translator cleared his throat, embarrassed. "She says, 'You cage me like a pig, but you are the pig.' The stuff before that, I don't think you want to hear." The translator was an intel captain, maybe twenty-two. A twenty-two-year old captain! With the war going the way it was, promotions came easy these days. Like Medals of Honor. The kid scuffed the floor with his boots. "This is all standard stuff, sir, just like last time," the translator said. "Not pleasant."

McCreary nodded. "I found her tied to a bed, you see. Back home. That Soviet general—"

"I'm sorry, sir," the kid said. "I've got interrogations at sixteen hundred. I can stay another five minutes, maybe." The translator knew the story. Everyone on base did.

McCreary felt the tears welling up. He shook them off. He stood, stepped toward Sunny's cage, and gripped the bars. "You can be normal again, Sunny! You can be an American! You're safe! Surrounded by the entre First Infantry—and the First Armored is on its way—"

Behind him, the kid cleared his throat. McCreary turned his head. The young officer shook his head. Meanwhile, Sunny lunged at the bars. McCreary moved his head away, weary but quick. His wife clawed the air inches from his downcast face. McCreary stepped toward his desk, hands in his hair. He'd blown it again. McCreary knew the rules. General Pearce let Sunny live, let her sleep in his quarters, even. But as long as Sunny spoke and acted Russian … she *was* Russian. That's why she remained in a cell, to which McCreary had no key. All she spoke anymore was that Mongol language, and no one really thought that she could understand the King's English. But that didn't matter. McCreary was never to talk to her about anything more serious than the weather.

He couldn't take any more. He covered his face. His Texas resolve gave way. He burst through the door of his tent. Too much. All of it: the bloody battle for his hometown, the treachery of Hawker—*Hawkerov.* And now, his caged wife, a loyal daughter of the Motherland.

McCreary reached to his chest and felt the medal that hung around his neck. He felt the star's sharp points dig into his fingers. And his soul.

McCreary ended up behind the fuel depot. He sat on an empty drum, staring at the new oak leaf on his cap. It glinted in the late afternoon Wyoming sun. All around him men ran between the command tents. Men with purpose. The way he'd been once. No, that wasn't quite right—they were panicked, the way they'd been since previous year, since the start of the war. All the bridges McCreary and his men had blown, all the Russian camps wiped out, all the gulags liberated—none of it was amounting to much. Ivan just kept comin'.

The ground below McCreary's toes shook. He raised his head to the sky. Five F-16s roared southwest, a menacing diagonal line. Loaded with ordnance. Headed for the front lines near Boulder, or Steamboat Springs. How many would survive their sorties? As if in answer, here came three straight-wing A-10s on their return trip. Shot to hell. Those birds had gone *mano y mano* with an armored column rumbling along Interstate 70. Half hadn't made it back. One A-10 was missing half its tail. The pilot leaned on one whining turbofan, then the other, struggling to keep the beast in the air.

Sunny was lost, but maybe she had the right idea. Maybe it was time for them all to learn a little Russian.

"There you are, Major!" Here came LaRoy, loping toward him from behind the latrines. "I been lookin' all over for you!" McCreary could see that even in BDUs he was shined, pressed, and polished. His new Silver Star glinted in the sun. Since being promoted to sergeant, LaRoy was motivated and squared away. "Major, you look lonelier than a schoolhouse in summertime!" But LaRoy knew the story. "Don't worry, sir," he said. "She'll come around."

"What can I do for you, Sergeant?"

"They want to see you, sir," LaRoy said. He was all perked up like a hunting dog, containing his excitement not at all. "While we were at that half-assed ceremony, General Pearce said all officers on deck! You're late!"

McCreary hopped off the oil drum and scuffed at the dirt.

"It sounds big, Major," LaRoy said. "He said it was time for this division to win the whole goddamn war!"

*   *   *

24

It was something McCreary never would get used to: when you won the Medal of Honor, your commanders saluted *you*. McCreary stepped into the dim command tent, to find no fewer than thirty officers, most outranking him, standing at attention. Under his shirt, the ribbon tugged at his neck. It was too heavy. This was too much for an ordinary boy from East Texas.

"Major McCreary," Pearce said. "It's high time you got the recognition you deserved. I'm sorry we missed the ceremony." He stepped forward and offered his hand. McCreary shook it.

"Aw, that's all right, General. You didn't miss much. Coupla' brass hung the darn thing around my neck, took a couple pictures, and flew back to Rapid City."

"Just be glad we're not fighting the *last* World War," Pearce muttered. "Damn fools would have carted you around Unoccupied America to sell war bonds."

He led McCreary to a large rectangular table, where the other men had gathered. The only light came from a row of naked overhead bulbs. Outside the tent, a generator thudded. The table under the bulbs was tiled with maps and charts. A dozen enlisted men listened to headphone chatter—friendly and otherwise—and nudged at red and blue plastic tiles with long sticks.

"As I was saying," Pearce intoned, "we've acquired what we believe are plans for Ivan's knockout punch: a full-scale invasion of Alaska next spring." He unrolled a large, three by four foot aerial photograph of scorched, mountainous terrain across the table's bare corner. "This film was inside the belly of a MiG we shot down two days ago. Division intelligence noticed these numbers here, here… and also here. Using one of the Soviet codes that we broke last month, we produced this." Pearce flipped the paper over and revealed a new image. McCreary made out a map. It showed two irregular shapes on opposite ends of the table, separated by white. Numbers dotted the map, sprinkled around two small splotches in the middle. Islands. Two line segments, accompanied by blocks of neat, Cyrillic text, joined the opposite ends of the chart. "The Bering Strait," General Pearce said. "This is the tip of Siberia. That's the Seward Peninsula in Alaska. The two Diomede Islands are here in the middle, anchor points."

A light colonel to McCreary's right leaned forward, astonished. "They're building a *bridge*. Can they… do that?"

"They can," Pearce said. "And they are. We believe there are three Soviet Army groups in and around Provideniya, just across the strait in Far East Siberia. But we've got most of Ivan's air assets tied up here over the States. He has neither the ships nor the fuel reserves for another naval operation. Without all that, there'd be no way to get those men, tanks, and equipment across the water. Until now."

Pearce fell silent to let this sink in. McCreary hung his head. Maybe it was the sight of his wife, caged like an animal and spitting at him. This, plus the prospect of the Soviet armies streaming through the roof of America, made any faint hope of winning this terrible war melt away. All was lost.

But if the war was over, someone had forgotten to let Pearce in on the news. "Men, there's hope," he said. "Lead elements of the First Armored Division will be here before midnight, with the rest arriving throughout the week. Colonel Greene and I will combine and reorganize into one corps. All of you are here because you will be given brigades and regiments. We will take most of what we have north, to stop these godless—"

A commotion interrupted Pearce's speech. Someone yanked the door open, framed into shadow by the sunlight. "You can't go in there!" said a young lieutenant, reaching to pull a tall figure back outside. McCreary reached for his Beretta M9. Before he could even get it out, the man casually raised his hands and spoke: "I couldn't help overhearing you all the way outside, General," he said, still in shadow. "So I'll just come out and say it: this... *Superbridge*... is a farce."

"Who the hell are you?"

The man stepped into the glow of the lamps. He was in his early forties, movie-star handsome, with thick, black hair. He wore pressed trousers, civvie hiking boots, and a sleeveless safari jacket over a flannel shirt. "I'm John Alexander, Central Intelligence Agency," the man said, resting his hands on the opposite end of the table. "That's fine security you have for your staff, General. I just walked right in here. I should kill you all, just to prove a point."

Most of the officers in the tent either had their hands on their Berettas, or held the pistols at their sides outright. Pearce looked to his left and his right.

"At ease," he grumbled.

"Yes, yes, all of you can rest easy," Alexander smirked. "I'm from the provisional federal government in South Dakota. I've been sent here under orders of Acting U.S. President Marshall."

"Tom Marshall? What does that old hog farmer want?"

"He wants me to talk some sense into you," Alexander said.

"If President Marshall's got a problem with how I'm handling this war—" Pearce looked up and down the row of his steel-jawed commanders "—then he can come out here in the weeds and run it himself."

But Alexander wasn't interested. The CIA man reached into his safari jacket and pulled out a blue plastic envelope the size of a license plate. "My credentials, General—and a request for you to hear me out. Nothing more."

Pearce leaned across the corner of the table and snatched the envelope away. He pulled a small metal tab from around his neck. With a faint crack, the plastic split open. The general removed and opened a tri-folded sheet of heavy stationery. The embossed presidential seal glinted. Pearce glanced over the letter, before handing it to Colonel Greene to his right.

As he waited, Alexander surveyed the charts and the colored pieces being nudged across the table. "I must say," Alexander said, "sending the Tenth Mountain west to fight to the last man in the Rockies while you sit here playing board games is doing wonders for Soviet morale."

"You've got three minutes!" Pearce barked. "Make 'em count."

"Certainly," Alexander said. "We understand that the First Armored Division is going to link up with you here within hours."

"That's right, what about it?"

"For once the president is happy about your waffling and indecision. You've given yourself time to make a good choice for once."

Colonel Greene started toward Alexander, but General Pearce held Greene's elbow and smiled. The general swept his other hand over his corner of the table. "Mr. Alexander, things have changed. We've figured out the entire Soviet strategy."

"Oh? And how did you manage that?" Alexander asked.

McCreary already didn't like Alexander. Not one bit.

"We shot down a MiG-31R near the Colorado border two days ago," Pearce said. He held up a corner of the chart. "He was in a hurry. Ferrying a coded schematic from their corps of engineers in Mexico City up to Alaska. Ivan will be driving tanks on a bridge across the Bering Strait by next year. If we allow that, you and the president may as well pack up and move the Free World to the moon."

Alexander had been nodding toward the end of the General's speech. Now he broke in: "Yes, General, this... unfortunate MiG of yours. Do you know who was flying it?"

Pearce turned to the three officers to his right. Greene fumbled and leafed through a manila folder. But before he could speak, Alexander started in himself, from memory:

"Colonel Vasily Fyodorov, born 1934 in Kiev. Graduated from the Soviet air academy in '55. Bottom of his class. But he bagged two of our jets in Korea and later scored five kills over Vietnam. In the first week of *this* war, he shot down six F-15s over Northern California. He had a wife back home in Sevastopol, plus another two in Mexico. Since the start of the war, he'd learned Spanish, and enjoyed reciting the poetry of—"

"Why don't you tell us what size underwear he had on?" Colonel Greene asked. Someone snickered.

"That's an excellent question, Colonel," Alexander said. "Fyodorov stood about five-foot-eight. And if he was built like a typical Ukrainian, I'd say he was a 38 large." Alexander paused and watched the red creep up from Greene's collar. "Can I continue?"

Greene fumed.

"Now pay attention, General. Fyodorov had two health conditions—Condition One, he was a Slavic male. Which led to Condition Two: stage IV liver cancer, with advanced cirrhosis. When you shot him down, he had three weeks left to live." Alexander leaned in. "General, Vasily Fyodorov knew he was a dying man. He volunteered for a suicide mission. You're falling for a ruse. Soviet reinforcements aren't coming through Alaska."

Greene leaned his knuckles on the table. "Then tell us what Ivan's doing in the Soviet Far East with a half-million men!"

Alexander looked at the table, then back at the command staff. He stood straight and scratched the back of his head. "We don't know that yet."

The colonel snorted.

"Here are some other things you don't know," Pearce said. "You don't know what happened to the Chinese last year after the People's Liberation Navy took Hawaii. An entire flotilla vanished, and you don't know why! You also don't know why the Russians haven't touched Los Angeles. And you sure as hell don't know where the next Russian reinforcements are coming from. But we do. We've shot down most of their transport aircraft and sunk most of their surface navy, so they can't get their men across the strait. But if they build that goddamned bridge—"

Alexander grabbed the edge of the table hard and shifted hundreds of tiles. The startled radiomen glared. "General, the Russians have one token airborne brigade holding all of Alaska. They've done nothing with it since the beginning of the war. It's all part of this elaborate fantasy you've swallowed. If you send First Armored chasing some imaginary Soviet monument, we'll lose. Your men will find nothing up there but polar bears and igloos. Then the Russians will attack us again out of the south or Greenland or the goddamned Lincoln Tunnel, and we won't have any way of stopping them."

"They're building a Superbridge! This isn't just an invasion—this is *colonization!*"

"You listen to me," Alexander replied. "When General Briggs gets here, you send his division west before snow closes the passes. Get them through Utah and you'll win this war by November. Because there's no way those Cossacks can build a fifty-mile ocean bridge in the dead of winter."

Silence descended through the tent, punctuated by the distant thunder of tank fire. McCreary saw Pearce smile. The general's silver mustache widened like spreading frost. "Unless," Pearce said, "they've carted two hundred thousand American slaves up to Alaska."

Alexander blanched. "Two hundred what?"

"That's right. Last month, refugees started leaking through the lines near Missoula. They tell all kinds of stories about the Russians. What they're doing to the women, of course—and how they dragged every able-bodied male out of every city and town between San Francisco and Seattle. Packed 'em in cattle cars and Greyhound buses. Shipped 'em up through Vichy Canada, flying them from Fairbanks to Nome, one transport plane at a time. They've thrown them all into a giant gulag. Camp Zhukov, they're calling it."

Alexander was flustered. "Why haven't you shared this with the president?"

"I did," the general said. "He ignored me. Too busy listening to the CIA. Until two days ago, we didn't know what the Russians were up to—slaves, a prison camp, setting up a friendly government in Western Canada. Now we know!"

"That proves nothing."

"It proves that they've got the plans, they have expendable manpower, and by spring they'll have a highway across the strait all the way to Fairbanks and points south." Pearce glared at Alexander over the tops of his glasses. "Now, Mr. Alexander, will that be all?"

Alexander straightened. "Maybe it will, General," he said. Pearce had rattled him. But McCreary knew that men like Alexander didn't lose their starch for long. "I should call the president," the CIA man said. "I need access to a radio and an operator with Yankee White clearance."

"Fourth tent on the right." Pearce spun the plastic envelope with the presidential pass into Alexander's chest. It bounced off and clattered to the table. "Dial direct," Pearce grinned, "*and put it on my tab.*"

Most of the men in the room laughed. But McCreary's heart sank. When men like Alexander and Pearce tore at each other's throats, the war was lost.

Backing away from the table, Alexander picked up the pass and slid it inside his jacket. He offered Pearce a curt nod. Walking out the door, Alexander paused and turned. He sneered at Pearce, McCreary, and the rest of the officers in the tent. "Congratulations, gentlemen," he said. "You just won Alaska."

Dusk. The faint thump of artillery fire over the mountains. Occasional flashes competed with the sunset. McCreary leaned against the fat ponderosa pine next to the door of his tent and once more dragged his tired eyes over the orders that the young private had delivered. *Welcome aboard,* the general had scrawled in the margins. According to the printout, McCreary was no longer in the Air Force. Pearce had seen to that. Now, McCreary was a full-fledged Army major. He had been handed command of the newly formed 16th Infantry Regiment. Enclosed in the envelope was a wilted shoulder patch, emblazoned with the division's crimson 1. But in the fading light, McCreary could make out other spots of red on the patch, along with stray threads around the edges. McCreary wondered what soldier's body they'd cut this patch off.

So that was it. McCreary would be shipping out. To where, he didn't know. The CIA man had been right. No one knew what to do next. Maybe the Russians were building a Superbridge to Alaska. Maybe they weren't. But one thing was certain: maybe this year, or the next, the United States of America would lose this war.

McCreary's thoughts turned to Sunny, or whatever General Azov had trained her to call herself. As if on cue, from inside the tent, from inside her cage, Sunny began to sing. It was a lullaby. The song was faint. Beautiful. Sad.

In Russian.

"What do you mean, you're turning it down?" Pearce glared up at McCreary from his desk. "You can't turn down a command assignment. There's a war on!"

"That's why I'm requesting permission to go to Alaska. Alone."

"What the devil for?"

"The Superbridge, sir. I believe you're right, but that intel man seems pretty sure of himself. If we make the wrong decision…"

Pearce braced his fingers against his bald head. The war sure was taking it out of the old man. "To tell you the truth," Pearce said, "I'm not sure what to think anymore."

"I'll get up there in a hurry," McCreary said. "Get a peek at the Strait, scope the prison camp, maybe hop over the water to Ivan's back porch. Either way, I'll be back here with a detailed report in a week."

Pearce smirked. "A week. What if they've already started building the damn thing?"

McCreary smirked back: "Then I'll blow it up. Just like at Royal Gorge."

Pearce shook his head, almost overwhelmed: "That bridge was a one-lane tourist trap. This is entirely different."

"A week, General. That'll give you and our CIA friend time to figure out what to do," McCreary said. "If this is all a trick, I shouldn't have any trouble. But if you don't hear from me, assume I ran into Ivan and the bridge is a go. Then tell Alexander where to shove it, come up and kill as many Russians as you can."

"You gonna hitchhike all the way up there?"

"Loan me a Black Hawk and a pilot who don't care about comin' home alive. I can help fly in a pinch."

"Denied. The Bering Strait is three thousand miles away. A UH-60 has a range of thirteen hundred. It's snowing already. The answer is no."

"We'll scavenge for fuel. There's got to be some Canadians on either side of the lines who'll help us."

"What about the rest of your J.C. Penney outfit?"

"It doesn't exist no more. Keep Dunsmuir and his men. You can't spare 'em, and like you said, if there is a bridge, it's too big for them, anyway. LaRoy's gonna be a good NCO for you. No use wasting him. And last I heard, Whitefeather's still scalpin' Russians down Oklahoma way. Just let me go up and have a look."

The general studied the floor. "McCreary, bridge or no bridge, there's at least one Russian division waiting for you. That's a suicide mission."

McCreary didn't respond. He held Pearce's gaze. A few seconds passed. The general sighed. "That's the idea," Pearce said, "isn't it? If I refuse, I suppose you'll disobey orders again. And again." Pearce nodded at the hint of exposed ribbon around McCreary's neck. "But your wife..."

"She ain't my wife, General. Not no more. I've—I've decided that she's gone."

"That so," Pearce said, pouring from a bottle of Jack Daniels.

"Did they get any intel out of her?" McCreary asked.

Pearce shook his head. "She didn't say anything that you and your men didn't already tell us. Azov turned her into a good Russian wife. Nothing more. She's no-value. What do you propose?"

"After our business here is done tonight… I'll take care of the problem."

"How?"

"With all due respect, sir, it's my business. I'll head straight back to my tent and… handle things."

"That's a lot to ask of a man."

"If you'll arrange for the chopper and a pilot, I'll leave tomorrow at 04:00."

Pearce handed McCreary his whiskey. "I'm sorry it had to happen this way, Mike. We'll raise a glass to her. Then, you do what you have to do."

The two warriors, tapped glasses, drank and fell silent. McCreary lowered his head and felt the whiskey's burn.

"War is hell, Major," Pearce said. "I'm sure she was a good woman." The old man had tears in his eyes. "You can forget about that Italian peashooter of yours." He handed his holstered M1916 Colt .45 automatic to McCreary, then extended his hand. McCreary gripped it—and, as expected, felt the cold brass of a key.

* * *

McCreary pushed the barrel of Pearce's .45 between Sunny's delicate shoulder blades and shoved her forward into the field. After giving him the key to Sunny's cell, Pearce had made three promises. One, he would order every man on that side of the base to stay in their quarters starting at 23:00. Two, no one would investigate when they heard the .45. And finally, in the morning, a simple unmarked patch of fresh, bare dirt would go undisturbed. The Army would treat Sunny's grave as sacred ground.

Now, under a chorus of crickets, Sunny saw the hole and the mound of dirt in the light of the full moon. But it wasn't until she made out the stubby, collapsible army-issue entrenching tool buried in the mound that she paused. Sunny turned around, facing the barrel. She was gray shadow. She closed her eyes.

McCreary raised the pistol high above his head. He fired. Sunny flinched. Her eyes flew open. He fired again. And again. Shots echoed against the trees. The crickets cut off. McCreary holstered the pistol and reached forward. He gave his former wife a shove. *"Run! That way!"* he hissed. *"GO! GIT! Your people are in that direction!"*

Sunny stood stock-still. His stubborn wife was in there somewhere. She muttered at him in Russian. She pointed at the tents far behind them and held up her hands. McCreary didn't understand.

Exasperated, she lunged forward, grabbed his shoulders… and planted a quick kiss on his cheek.

McCreary's heart began to pound. Maybe—

"Spasibo," she whispered.

McCreary shoved her. She toppled backward into the grass. He pointed in the direction of the Russian lines. Standing over her, McCreary felt a confusing mix of sadness and anger…

Hatred.

Lust.

No! *None of that.* When Sunny didn't move, McCreary pulled his pistol out again. He fired into the ground two feet to the right of her head.

That was it. Sunny scrambled backward and stumbled to her feet, running through the high grass. At the edge of the trees, she paused, holding her skirt above her feet. She looked over her shoulder at him. After a lingering glance, she disappeared into the night.

With steadying hands, McCreary pulled the E-tool out of the mound and filled the hole.

04:00

The UH-60 Black Hawk's rotors spun and the turbines whined. McCreary shifted the gear on his shoulders and tried to reach for his orders, but the guards stood at attention on sight. McCreary nodded and waved. He walked past the guardhouse onto the pad. The ground crew was almost done saddling up the UH-60. As McCreary approached, one of them slid open the side door. McCreary tossed in his gear, removed his cover, and tossed it onto the floor of the Black Hawk. The crewman stowed his rifle and slid the door shut. McCreary climbed into the cockpit and pulled on his helmet. It had been a while.

The pilot was black, with a thin, Army-issue mustache. "Charles Washington?" McCreary asked into the mic.

"Warrant Officer 5 Charles Washington to be exact, sir!" the pilot said. He offered his hand. McCreary shook it.

"General Pearce tells me we're going on a little hop up north!" Washington said.

"That's right!"

"It'll be my pleasure, sir! My entire family was visiting my brothers in D.C. when the missiles hit. My wife, my pop, my mamma, even my little brother Tyrone. All gone. It's payback time."

Washington had a score to settle. McCreary had asked for a depressed pilot—suicidal, maybe. Not one with a vendetta.

"All right, we gotta lay track over as much of Free Canada as we can," McCreary said as strapped in. "Time's wasting!" But the pilot was leaning forward, looking off to McCreary's right. McCreary turned. Two men—one towering and one of average height—sprinted toward the chopper, M-16A2s at their sides. Laden with gear. Both wore bushwhacker hats and had painted lines under their eyes. The smaller man had an awkward, loping stride—it was clear that LaRoy wanted to come along. And the big man towering next to him... no...

Impossible!

McCreary ripped the helmet off his head, threw open the door. He lurched out of the Black Hawk. He ran to Sergeant Charles Whitefeather and grabbed both his shoulders. He wanted to shake him, but the big Indian was too sturdy to move.

"What—? How—?"

Whitefeather smiled. "Thank the spirit winds, Major!"

"But—"

"I left the Cherokee Brigade and hitched a ride up with the First Armored," Whitefeather said in his rich baritone. "I knew you were going to the home of the winter gale long before you did."

This wasn't in the mission profile. McCreary and the pilot wouldn't be coming back. He turned to LaRoy. "Both of you get away from this chopper! That's an order!"

"We all heard about Sunny, Major," LaRoy said. "Puttin' her down had to be tough to do. But it weren't your fault! We gotta give Ivan a beat-down." McCreary opened his mouth to reply, but what could he say? And Whitefeather's face—so sad! "You wanna keep us off this detail," LaRoy continued, "you'll have to shoot us!"

Damn it all. No time. He swore, turned, and pulled open the UH-60's side door. "Get in there, you knuckleheads, before I change my mind!" Whitefeather and LaRoy smiled at each other and clambered aboard the Black Hawk.

He got back in the front seat. Washington was still looking off to the right. *What now?*

A tall man in a safari jacket, laden with gear, argued with the guards. In his left hand, he gripped the midsection of a Heckler & Koch MP5, strap dangling. Pure CIA. The man gestured with it toward McCreary and the chopper. But the guards weren't hearing it. John Alexander reached into his jacket and produced a banded sheet of paper, one of those computer printouts with dots up and down either edge. He shoved it toward the younger guard's face. The kid held it up, trying to capture some of the light coming from the guardhouse. After a moment, he handed the CIA man's orders back to him and shooed him toward the Black Hawk.

"Aw, what the heck is this?" McCreary exclaimed. He was going to order Washington to lift off but he was too slow. Alexander was already at McCreary's door, holding his orders against the glass. McCreary didn't feel like fishing out his flashlight. He jerked his thumb back to the side door. McCreary sagged in his seat and pointed upward once he knew the door was shut. "All right, Charlie, get us out of here before the whole division shows up." Washington snorted into his mic.

Like a giant insect, the Blackhawk lifted off the pad and turned. McCreary's stomach dropped into his hips. Already he could make out both bases below his feet, Army and Air Force. Row upon row of camouflaged tents and netted fighter planes. America's dwindling hope. McCreary wondered about Sunny and where she was, how she would survive. But she was on her own.

Off at the big base, a hodgepodge of jets—F-18s, F-15s, surplus A-4s, Navy gray and Air Force blue— lined up with blinking runway lights to take their turn at Ivan. And glory be: there were the spinning propellers of a pair of taxiing A-1 Skyraiders, loaded with bombs under their straight wings. Where in the hell had the Air Force unearthed those dinosaurs? Were things that bad?

And there was Interstate 25, lined to the south with the tanks and trucks of the incoming First Armored Division, America's last hope. As Washington turned the helicopter toward the north, McCreary said a silent prayer for the pilots, the soldiers, and the tattered nation itself. He leaned back in his seat and closed his eyes.

Washington dipped the Black Hawk's nose. The great silent chopper drove forward toward darkness, Canada, and the trouble to come.

DAY TWO

Sept. 22, 1989
A UH-60 Black Hawk
50 feet over Free Canada

Forest had given way to the soft carpet of endless Canadian fields—silver waves of grass mixed with last year's winter wheat. McCreary thought about what the starving people in Chicago or Kansas City could do with that wheat. The chopper sailed over it so fast, quiet, and low that McCreary wanted to open the cockpit door and drag his boots along the tops. Instead, he reread Alexander's abridged orders, direct from the top:

CONFIRMATION ROMEO OSCAR NOVEMBER

CHARLIE TANGO-TANGO LIMA ALPHA 220040 DELTA LIMA

CENTCOM—SOUTH DAKOTA

--> MCCREARY, M., MAJ. U.S. ARMY

CDR, OPERATION ICEPICK

CENTRAL INTEL AGENT ID 8723 BRAVO

ATTACHED IN ADVISORY ROLE

AFFORDED FULL PASSAGE AND PRIVILEGES

EXECUTIVE ORDER, SIGNED BY MY HAND

McCreary tore the paper into thin strips, made confetti, then stuffed the little blizzard out his side window. "Major McCreary," Alexander's voice intoned over McCreary's headset, "I see that your poorly written mission profile doesn't have many refueling drops. Did the forecast over the Yukon call for showers of JP-8?"

McCreary monitored the fuel gauges just fine. He didn't have time for Alexander's arrogance. "Mr. Alexander," he said, "I'm ordered to take you along, not to listen to your second-guessin'."

"That's where you're wrong, Major. According to the President of the United States, my … *second-guessin'* is precisely what you're required to listen to."

"General Pearce gave me five possible refueling spots," McCreary shot back. "The best one is a satellite tracking station in friendly hands. It was transmitting codes free and clear when we took off. It's at least a hundred and fifty miles east of the fighting. Now shut up and stay off the intercom!"

The CIA man wouldn't quit. "There was a raid not far from that station last week. Spetsnaz unit—Russian special forces. The other two sites came under Occupied Canadian control in August. And that oil station was taken out by a Katyusha rocket attack. So, four of your five waypoints no longer exist, which leaves you with one that may be in Russian hands by now." Alexander chuckled. "I haven't seen such sloppy intel since the Trojan Horse."

McCreary looked at Washington, who kept his hands on the throttle and stick. The pilot shrugged.

"Fortunately," Alexander went on, "I have two other waypoints with enough fuel to get us all the way to Kamchatka. The first is a CIA outpost thirty klicks north of Spruce Grove. I'm one of thirteen men on earth who knows that it exists."

Washington pulled a plastic chart out of his visor and checked it over. He put his thumb against the likely location. McCreary could see it was too far north. But maybe there was something to what Alexander was saying. The thin, spread-out lines in this sector were too fluid. The Free Canadians were giving the Russians and their traitorous Vancouver allies the what-fer, but the dance was chaotic. Most of the combat was hand-to-hand. Who knew where the lines were? Washington looked back at McCreary and shrugged. He shook his head.

"The satellite station is good, Mr. Alexander," McCreary said. "Now sit back and zip it."

But Alexander poked his head into the cockpit and dropped a new chart into the pilot's lap, laminated and folded into threes. Then he turned to McCreary. The rising sun reflected in his CIA issue sunglasses. "You listen to me, Major," he shouted over the turbines. "If you hope to get within five hundred miles of the Seward Peninsula in one piece, you'll do as you're told."

McCreary already had enough. He jabbed his finger at Alexander's chest. "You get your behind back there and shut up! LaRoy, Whitefeather: help this yahoo find his seat!"

Alexander ignored him and turned to Washington. The spy grabbed the pilot's shoulder. The Black Hawk dipped. McCreary unhooked his harness and spun. He caught the front of Alexander's safari jacket and threw him into the back. LaRoy and Whitefeather were unhooking themselves; they caught the CIA man before he tumbled into the rack of M-16s. Whitefeather ripped off Alexander's headset. The spy's sunglasses went flying. By the time LaRoy shoved him into one of the seats along the bulkhead, Alexander was blinking in the morning sun.

"'That spook says one more thing," McCreary shouted, "you throw him over the side!" The last thing McCreary saw from the back was Whitefeather handing Alexander's sunglasses back to him.

In the cockpit, McCreary strapped in. Washington piped up: "I don't like that guy either, Major, but he may be right about that station."

"The satellite station was broadcasting the code before we took off," McCreary said. "You said so yourself."

"That was all automated. I've tried popping them twice over the mic since our guest started in about Spruce Grove," the pilot said. "They should have popped us back. Not a sound."

"Maybe they have a down transmitter."

Washington glared at him from behind his visor: "Or maybe the new owner has a funny accent."

McCreary checked Alexander's charts. His substitute refueling spots were marked in red exes 900 miles apart. No deal. "These are even closer to the lines. Too risky. Besides, I don't trust that son of a bitch."

Washington smirked behind his visor. "What in this world can we trust anymore?"

McCreary resumed scanning the overgrown fields and muddy bogs passing under the chopper. "My gut," he said, *"and nothin' else."*

* * *

The satellite-tracking dish rose over the horizon twenty miles out. The plains had given way to a scattering of small trees and lakes, carved out of the rocky soil by glaciers long ago. There was already six inches of snow on the ground. McCreary could feel the cold through the glass. By the time the collection of low cinderblock buildings came into view, the three men in back were peering forward between the seats.

And from the station, neither Washington nor McCreary had heard a sound.

Whitefeather: "I don't like this, Major."

Washington flew them over the station's fuel dump, pyramids of blue drums. The station's chopper stood chained nearby. McCreary could see an ancient fuel truck parked next to it. There was no snow on either of the vehicles. Lacy patterns of footprints all around. Someone had used them today.

"That's our go-juice," Washington said. "All the equipment's ready to go. Only… no people."

"How convenient," Alexander said. "Let me guess: we don't have enough fuel to try someplace else."

McCreary didn't answer. He looked at Washington and spun his finger around in a circle. *One more pass.* But the UH-60's low fuel alarm began to whine. Washington shook his head. "Fumes."

"Can we get this thing refueled in ten minutes?"

"With a buddy I can do it in five." That'd be one less gun. "Alexander, you're gonna help Washington," McCreary said.

"You're not using me in the proper capacity," Alexander replied. "I had seventeen sniper kills in Vietnam—"

"Mr. Alexander, last warning. Shut up and do as I say." Washington spun the Black Hawk toward the fuel dump. Nothing below them moved. "Worst-case, the Russians cleaned it out and moved on," McCreary told them. "If it's an ambush, they'd have shot us down by now."

"Unless they want this chopper in one piece," Alexander intoned. "Don't land here, McCreary."

"Doors open on my mark," McCreary said. "Alexander, I want thirty-four hundred liters of premium and a clean windshield. Whitefeather, right side. LaRoy on the left. Stay close, full sweep. If anything moves cut it in half."

McCreary checked Pearce's .45 and pointed it at the floor. He undid his harness with his free hand.

"Open her up!" he ordered the men in back. He pulled off his helmet.

The pilot set the Black Hawk down less than thirty feet from the barrels. McCreary's boots hit the tarmac a half second later, with LaRoy creeping along behind him. McCreary had his .45 up and sweeping the row of three equipment sheds. Each was untouched. Not even a broken window. The last had its sliding door ajar. Footprints went in and out of the buildings. No sounds, other than LaRoy's fading, crunching footsteps. Behind McCreary, the UH-60's rotor slowed to a stop. Silence descended.

McCreary looked over his left shoulder. Alexander had attached the hose to the Black Hawk, hands shaking, his HK slung over his shoulder. The CIA man looked everywhere but the chopper. He looked scared. McCreary smiled to himself. *Good.* Washington checked the truck's gauges. Thumbs up. JP was flowing. McCreary stepped forward and took up position behind a rusted forklift. He ached for his M-16A2 back in the chopper and the grenade launcher slung under its

46

barrel. Too late for that. Besides, he'd been shooting a pistol since he was eight.

McCreary heard a faint whistle. Whitefeather. The Indian jerked his head sideways at a one of the sheds. Whitefeather had… that look. He crept forward through the snowy grass to the shed's sliding door, his own M-16A2 rough and ready. The door was ajar two or three feet. The Indian glanced at McCreary, then picked a baseball-sized rock out of the snow. Standing to the right of the door, he pitched it in. The rock clanged against metal, then skid across concrete.

Whitefeather tilted his head; it wasn't the result he'd been expecting. The big Indian shrugged, turned, and crept away. Then he grunted and sank to one knee. Whitefeather wheeled and without aim fired a burst with his M-16 into the shed.

A stocky, white-uniformed torso slumped forward, headless, spraying blood into the snow. In the corpse's hand, McCreary could see the bladeless hilt of a gas-propelled knife.

Spetsnaz.

The fuel depot came alive with a crisscross of tracers.

McCreary instinctively hit the ground against a furious shower of AK fire. He looked to the chopper. Alexander had disappeared, leaving the fuel hose connected to the Black Hawk. McCreary could see Washington's boots motionless under the fuel truck. Meanwhile, Whitefeather had pulled himself to a sitting position. With a warrior's cry, he fired a round from his M203 into the center shed. It streaked into the open door. McCreary planted his face into the snow. After a split second delay, the M433 High-Explosive Dual Purpose Round exploded. In an open field, the HEDP caused casualties within a 130-meter radius, and had a kill radius of five meters. The sound was a clap of thunder. The frozen ground under McCreary's body bounced him six inches into the air.

McCreary lifted his face in time to see five men in white snowsuits flee the third shed. The men who'd been inside were panicked, tripping and staggering through the second shed's debris. In each of their hands was an AK-47.

McCreary rose to his knee, brought up the general's .45, and began firing. After years of using the Baretta, the .45's more powerful recoil was like wrestling with the devil himself. McCreary missed the first three shots, but adjusted. In a jerking dance of arms, set to the music of Russian cries, each of the five men fell one by one. Dead before they hit the ground.

Behind McCreary, the sound of automatic weapons fire hadn't abated. There was still the first shed. As he turned, McCreary took in two alarming sights: a disabled Soviet BTR-60 armored personnel carrier, its turret knocked aside like a jaunty cap, all of it surrounded by the remains of the center shed. And, lying before all of it was Whitefeather's huge, prone, outstretched body, his M-16A2 at his side. The proud warrior had destroyed the BTR-60, the shed the Russians had parked it in, and quite possibly himself.

Automatic fire poured out of the first shed's broken windows, bright orange tracers in the evening gloom. McCreary sprinted to the chopper. He reached the Black Hawk and found it in one piece, though some errant shots had clouded the bullet resistant cockpit windows. He climbed through the open side door and found his M-16. Loaded, with another M433 in the grenade launcher. McCreary hopped out, holstered his pistol and crept toward the first shed.

But he'd missed the party. Still a hundred feet away, McCreary saw a bright orange flash blow out the shed's remaining windows. He heard the thump a second later, and then was blown back when the entire building disintegrated. McCreary landed on his back, stunned. He rolled to his stomach and retrieved his rifle. But the firing had stopped. All around him looked like the remains of a butcher shop. God knew how many Commies. The Russians were dead now, thanks to LaRoy, somehow, somewhere. He turned and surveyed the scene back at the chopper. There was Whitefeather, still motionless in the snow. Washington was no longer under the fuel truck. The Black Hawk's rotors started to spin in a slow circle.

"*NE DVIGAT'SYA!*" McCreary heard a deep, powerful voice behind him. "Yankee! Drop rifle! Or I shoot you in your imperialist *yagoditsy*, yes?"

McCreary froze and dropped his M-16.

"Turn now and face proud Russian warrior before you die!" To this, the Russian added: "*I shit on Thomas Jefferson!*"

McCreary turned. His captor emerged from a stack of faded, pitted tires.

See you on the other side, Sunny.

The Russian was hatchet-faced, with a black beard and heavy Georgian eyebrows. Even in the scant light, McCreary could see that the man's white fatigues were stained faint red. Whom had he killed—?

The Russian's face disappeared in a pink mist. His body froze; two eyes dangled from the exposed skull by their optic nerves. The body then went limp as the puppetmaster cut the strings. The man folded into the snow.

Alexander's voice: "Move it, McCreary! Before you mess this up any further!" McCreary scooped up his rifle. Alexander sprinted a few yards ahead of him. And way ahead was LaRoy, with Whitefeather slung over his shoulders in an absurd display of hillbilly strength. But over the sudden whir of the Black Hawk's rotors, something wasn't right. McCreary slowed to a walk, then stopped. He turned, tuning his ear to the faint sounds from across the compound.

"McCreary!"

McCreary raised his hand toward the chopper, hoping to shut Alexander up. LaRoy threw Whitefeather's inert form into the chopper. At least those two would get away.

"McCreary, goddammit!"

McCreary sprinted toward the main compound and the giant satellite dish. It loomed over him with every step. Before him lay more buildings, certainly with more Russians, alerted to his presence. A few yards shy of the main gate, McCreary launched himself into the snow.

What was that sound?

A male voice, panicked and high pitched:

"Povtoryayu! My nakhodimsya pod atakoy! Amerikantsy zdes' i unichtozhili firmy A i V! Zapros podkrepleniye! My ne znayem, chto delat'! Povtorite!"

The voice came from inside one of the smaller, cinderblock buildings under the dish. A scared Russian radio operator pleading with superiors for some kind of help. Without thinking, McCreary raised the M-16A2 and fired his armor-piercing grenade at the dish. In the faint light, he couldn't trace the grenade itself. The glowing gray vapor trail arced toward the giant saucer. But the round skipped off the dish with a hollow thud— then spun down toward the buildings, where it exploded with a blinding flash. He'd hit something back there. Explosives. Fuel. Something big.

The ground shook again. McCreary staggered to his feet and ran back toward the chopper. Behind and above him he heard a malevolent groan. McCreary glanced over his shoulder to see the dish crashing to earth a few yards behind him. The giant scoop of air threw him forward again. A chain of explosions, each more powerful than the last lit up the sky. McCreary struggled to his feet. He made it to the chopper a few seconds later. Washington was lifting off before McCreary's boots were even inside the Black Hawk.

The only thing louder than the rotors were the control panel alarms, a symphony of them. McCreary rolled on his back, squashed flat by the upward acceleration. Everywhere he looked, the bird was full of holes.

19:35
Northern British Columbia

The Black Hawk rested in the clearing. Whitefeather had regained consciousness but he was only fifty percent, as Alexander sewed the wound in his back. Washington crept around the chopper in the snow, shivering in his flight suit and hoping in vain to find the source of a troubling oil leak with his flashlight. God knew how many rounds had punched his proud bird.

McCreary patrolled the edge of the clearing, wearing his AN/AVS 6 ANVIS night vision system. There was nothing out there in the trees but a sea of green and black. "That was a fancy ass knife," he heard LaRoy say.

"*Spetsnaz*, all right," Washington said, peering at the tail rotor. "Some James Bond shit, right there." LaRoy tossed the knife to McCreary, who lifted his goggles and examined the hilt in the faint glow of the cockpit lights.

51

He saw steel, Cyrillic characters, and death. McCreary tossed it into the trees.

"Oh how deluded we are in these troubled times," Alexander said from the back of the open chopper. "They weren't Spetsnaz. Those men were regular army. And poorly trained, I might add."

LaRoy chimed in: "Fella, you got yourself a big, know-it-all mouth, you know that?"

"Sergeant LaRoy, you're making me uncomfortable," Alexander said without emotion, sewing Whitefeather's back. "As excited as you may be to have me in the woods after dark, let's not talk about my mouth. As I was saying, the trick blade that got Sergeant Whitefeather here was fired by their political officer. The rest of those men we massacred were rear guard. The one I saved you from was a cook, McCreary. For Christ's sake."

As Alexander rambled, McCreary stashed his rifle, and moved to the front of the chopper in silence. Alexander didn't quit. "Do you know what that means, McCreary?" McCreary didn't answer. "Your selection of refueling stops didn't put us *close* to the occupied lines. This chopper and its quarter tank of fuel are now forty klicks *into* Occupied Canada." He tied off Whitefeather's wound and yanked down the Indian's shirt.

"You and I can agree or disagree about the Superbridge, Major," Alexander said, "but at least now the entire Soviet Army knows we're here."

DAY THREE

Sept. 23, 1989
A UH-60 Black Hawk
Juneau Ice Field

The chopper swooped through burnt orange cathedrals of ice and rock. McCreary awoke to find the Black Hawk surrounded by towering peaks and jagged, sagging crevasses. Whitefeather was awake, his earlier dazed expression replaced with his trademark hard scowl. Alexander peered through the windows, his glance sweeping to and fro across the forbidding landscape. Beside him, LaRoy snored, his head back, mouth open.

McCreary read the fuel gauges: at their current airspeed, the UH-60 would seize up and fall from the sky in a little under an hour. He didn't even want to think about their sinking oil pressure. McCreary pulled a chart from the visor and ran the numbers twice. They would run out of fuel thirty miles short of Juneau, their only hope. Whether the capital city was in Communist hands or forgotten by the Russian war machine, even Alexander didn't know. Two more alarms began to chime on McCreary's instrument panel. The engines were overheating. He turned to Washington, who held up his hand and shook his head.

Save it—I know.

Maybe that wasn't so bad. If they flew all the way into Juneau, the Black Hawk would attract attention. They could set down someplace hidden, and slip into the city unnoticed—

The explosion rocked the Black Hawk from behind. It pitched forward. Sparks and smoke filled the cockpit.

"Goddamn motherfucker!" Washington cried out. "RPG!" Alarms rang and shrieked and then fell silent as another explosion hit. McCreary clutched the roof, and the world began to spin, white and blue and orange, and then black.

McCreary awoke to snow, cold, and pain, lying on his side. He opened his eyes, wiped his face. A mix of snow and blood covered his forearm. As the world swam into focus, he saw that the Black Hawk hung over the edge of a bottomless, white precipice. McCreary reached for the door handle, then froze. Even that motion caused the chopper's wreckage to rock and groan. Besides, the door was gone.

He turned toward where Washington had been sitting. The pilot's side door was replaced by a jagged hole of sky. McCreary's gaze followed the twisted assembly of straps, taut, out the side of the chopper. He lifted his head, slowly, slowly, and saw Washington dangling by his chest. The pilot was awake, aware that he was moments from death.

"Oh, please, dear Jesus," Washington whispered. "Oh Jesus, please…"

"Washington!" McCreary hissed. "Don't move. I'm comin' for you!"

"No, no, no! *You* don't move! You freeze or the whole thing's gonna go, goddammit!"

McCreary heard LaRoy's voice. "Major! Sit still as a possum! We're gonna come get ya! Don't do nothin' crazy!" McCreary turned away from Washington's predicament to peer up the icy slope. The chopper had fallen into the side of this mountain and rolled, losing some of its hull and all of its glass. The Black Hawk's wreckage was hung up on ice-covered rocks, underlain by a powdery layer of snow. The slope was at least sixty degrees, and past the other side of the chopper, that slope fell away into space.

McCreary heard a creak behind him. He saw Alexander and Whitefeather scrambling past LaRoy up the slope. High above all three of them were spires of rock at least fifty feet up the rise. McCreary caught a hint of the Black Hawk's L4 Nylon Type 4 repelling lines trailing behind the three men. Even Alexander. God bless them.

"Washington," McCreary said, voice as even as he could keep it, "they're gonna secure us with lines. You just stay put. Don't look down, now."

The chopper slid another couple of inches and stopped. McCreary gripped what remained of the airframe. Snow swept past the Black Hawk. A small shower of rocks passed under the twisted hull. McCreary closed his eyes. This was what he'd wanted. An end to everything, to meet Sunny—

No!

He had a mission. The fate of the Republic rested upon him and this rag-tag bunch. There was no time to wait for the repelling lines. McCreary gingerly unhooked his harness. He turned toward Washington. The chopper stayed put as he moved himself toward the left side of the chopper. McCreary inched forward just a bit more. He met the dangling pilot's gaze.

Washington's panic was gone. His expression was peaceful. He even smiled. "Hey, Major. I'm afraid this is goodbye. I know you got a Ka-Bar. You cut me loose, you hear? If you don't, I'll take the whole mess down with me."

McCreary extended his hand. "Reach up! Washington! Dammit, man, that's an order!"

Instead, Washington smiled again. "Ain't no way for a black man to catch a break in this army. Guess I gotta do it myself." The pilot unsheathed his own knife, and sawed at the harness.

"You stop that right now, Washington!"

Washington didn't listen. He'd kept his knife sharp, like any good soldier. One by one, the straps holding him in his twisted, dangling seat popped free. With a few more cuts, only one strap remained, tangled around his shoulder.

Washington made eye contact with McCreary once more. "Good luck, sir! Give those Russian bastards a kick in the behind." He made the last cut and fell away. With his right hand, as he fell into the icy abyss, the pilot raised a crisp salute.

"NOOOOOOOOOOOOO!" McCreary yelled. And like that, Washington was gone—and the chopper rocked back the other way. Just then, McCreary felt two heavy arms land on his back, and yank him up out of the twisted beast, as the entire thing groaned back the other way. McCreary scrambled out of the chopper. With a long, awful scrape, the entire mess tilted and disappeared over the side.

Survival instinct kicked in. He and Whitefeather scrambled up, past a fusillade of snow and ice and rocks coming the other direction. They sprinted past the tangled, useless lines. Up ahead were trees. And there were boots. Boots belonging to LaRoy. And Alexander.

And…

And…?

McCreary made it to the top of the slope. A gloved hand met him, outstretched, its owner flanked by the bristling business ends of assault rifles. The man who hauled McCreary into captivity wore a white snowsuit, similar to the Soviets at the radar station. The stranger stood a trim six feet tall, with neat black hair, blue eyes, and a trim mustache. Cutting across his chest was a diagonal Sam Browne, affixed with the unmistakable silver insignia of Occupied Canada: a hammer, a sickle— and a maple leaf in place of the Soviet star.

"Good morning," the man said. "I am Colonel Mortimer Tremblay of the Democratic Workers' Federation of Canada, Special Forces Command. And you, Major Michael McCreary, have much explaining to do."

Two dozen men surrounded McCreary and his comrades. Half the men looked like more polite versions of American boys. These were the Canadians. The rest had the dirty, unshaven look of the Slavic horde. Their weapons were a mix of C7 assault rifles—the stockier cousin to the American M-16—and old, reliable AK-47s. Three of the Slavs held Soviet RPG-7s in both hands. It was a sickening display of international cooperation.

McCreary stood and offered Tremblay a salute. "Colonel," he said, "we seem to have wandered off the trail. Didn't mean to cause a fuss." Blood trickled into McCreary's eye. It stung. He didn't blink.

Tremblay returned McCreary's salute. He followed with a smirk and a nod at McCreary's hip. "Your sidearm, please." With regret, McCreary unbuckled General Pearce's holster and handed it over. Tremblay examined the stocky handgrip before handing it to a subordinate. "A Colt .45," he mused, "thuggish and antiquated. Why should I expect anything less from our neighbours to the south? Major McCreary, you are trespassing. Your presence in our airspace was a violation of our neutrality."

"Neutrality?" He nodded at Tremblay's bunch. "Aren't those some Russian fellas over there, mixed with your'n?"

"The Canadian civil conflict is an internal matter," Tremblay said. "Soviet Command warned us that an American strike team had massacred a radar station on Canadian soil. But you are curiously over-equipped for a simple raid. Our Russian friends are rather curious about your mission. So I ask again, why are you here?"

When McCreary didn't respond, Tremblay edged away. He stepped crisply on the steep slope toward Alexander. The spy stared at the ground. "And at long last: Agent Robert Alexander of the CIA," Tremblay said. He lifted Alexander's chin with a finger. Alexander jerked his head away. "Taking a break from torturing Nicaraguan villagers, I see. The KGB will be most interested to spend some time with you. Perhaps you and their interrogators can… catch up on old times, *eh?*"

Tremblay put his hands behind his back, and continued his review. "Sergeant LaRoy of the coal mines. Sergeant Whitefeather of the native reserve. Happy to see that you have avoided the unfortunate fate of Warrant Officer Washington, your brother in class and colour oppression. And yet, poor souls like you follow Uncle Sam's bugle call into battle again, and again, and again. For greed. For oil. Sergeant Whitefeather: how can you fight for these men who occupy the sacred land of your ancestors? When all our Russian partners desire is to give it back to you!"

Watching and listening, McCreary failed to follow the Canadian's logic. All this talk—and Tremblay didn't have a drop of Indian blood anywhere in him. McCreary expected Whitefeather to point this out. Instead, the Comanche intoned, "Indians join the U.S. Army to *protect* our land, Colonel. With all due respect, it looks like we could give you all a few pointers."

LaRoy snickered. Tremblay stood up straighter, glared at LaRoy, and back at McCreary. The Canadian stepped down the slope. Gravel slid past McCreary's feet, and off the cliff behind him. Somewhere in the distance, he heard the heavy blades of a Russian helicopter. "Under the laws of war, Major, I am within my rights to execute the lot of you as spies. Thanks to several well-placed assets back at your headquarters, we knew of your identities before you left Cheyenne. But we cannot fathom *what* you are doing here."

"Crashing," McCreary said.

Tremblay seethed. "Tell me what I wish to know, or this will be the *pro*-cess: we will throw you and your brave men over the cliff."

McCreary spat blood into the snow. He wasn't going to tell this Canadian a thing. Tremblay breathed through his nose. He glanced at McCreary's neck and reached out. He snagged the ribbon and tugged the medal from his collar before letting it fall against his chest. "The Medal of Honor," he said. "How many helpless Russian and Mexican conscripts had to die for that trinket?" He put his hands on McCreary's shoulders, raised his knee, and brought it into his solar plexus.

McCreary dropped to his knees. He squeezed two handfuls of snow and rock, ready to throw it into Tremblay's beady Canadian eyes—but thought better of it. He found his breath and looked up. "Colonel, if you're going to shoot us, just get it over with," he said. "There's a war on."

Tremblay smiled. "Indeed there is—one you will lose by November." The Canadian brought his boot around and caught McCreary in the face. Once more, McCreary knew little else but cold, and pain. The last image he saw before passing out was the spires of rock pointing to the sky—and the shadowy form of a hulking, Soviet Mli Mi-24 Hind helicopter, descending on them like a spider.

13:30
An Mli Mi-24 Hind helicopter
500 feet

McCreary awoke in the Hind's windowless troop compartment. There was faint yellow light from a row of flickering lamps overhead. He was bound, back-to-bulkhead, head forward. Lifting it was agony. He looked down between his knees and saw vomit between his boots.

LaRoy sat to his left, bound; across the way sat Whitefeather, staring ahead, and Alexander, across from McCreary. Alexander had been staring at him.

"Well, well," Alexander sneered. "Our fearless leader is awake. I see they let you keep your Medal of Honor. Very kind of our Canadian hosts. I wonder how the Soviets will treat you."

"We'll find out soon enough," McCreary said. "Unless we come up with a way out of this."

Whitefeather smiled. "You never give up, Major," he said. "That's why LaRoy and I will follow you to the ends of the earth."

McCreary managed half a grin, but lowered his head again. It weighed twenty pounds. "Who's got an idea? I ain't got the luxury of rejecting any plan. We'll be on the ground in Vancouver soon."

Alexander chuckled. "No we won't. Feel that rattle? That's ocean turbulence. We're flying over the Gulf of Alaska. Probably to that slave camp General Pearce mentioned."

"How do you know so much about everything, Mr. Alexander?" McCreary asked. "You one of them double agents?"

Alexander smiled. "Says the man who let his brainwashed, Russian-speaking wife slip away toward the Soviet lines, with information about troop strength, equipment, and the location of division headquarters."

All three members of Lonestar Tactical Unit One sat up straight.

"That's right, gentlemen," Alexander said. "You heard how the proud major sacrificed his wife for country and duty, with a humane bullet to the back of her pretty head. But he didn't kill her. No—he let her go."

"That's ... that's a damn lie!" McCreary said.

"Except that I was outside Pearce's tent when you offered to lead this mission to Alaska," Alexander said. "After that, I followed you to the sad, wooded clearing with Sunny—or was that Svetlana?"

"Don't you dare—"

"General Yuri Azov was a pioneer of intracranial reprogramming," Alexander said. "He ran a secret lab in Kamchatka twenty years before he turned up in your hometown of"—he added in a dead-on impression of McCreary's slow drawl—"*Wrangler Plains, Texas.*"

"You shut your goddamned CIA mouth!"

"And yesterday, you denied my requests for a safer waypoint, leading us into a Soviet ambush. If you'd listened to me, we'd be in one piece right now. Or, would you have found another opportunity to deliver me to your new bosses in Alaska?" Alexander shook his head. "This whole ruse about the Superbridge," he said. "Boys, I'll lay ten-to-one odds that when we land at Camp Zhukov, we'll find nothing but a KGB ops center. Then, Major McCreary will make sure that you two are shot in the back of the head over a shower drain. I'll be handed over for interrogation. And then, he'll radio a fanciful report back to division headquarters in Cheyenne. Pearce and Briggs will bring all of their forces to Alaska, just in time for the second Soviet wave to hit the U.S. from Mexico or Greenland. That is, if Major McCreary's wife didn't win the war for the Russians already."

"I'm an American soldier! I killed five men back at that station!"

"You Communists are nothing if not ruthless," Alexander replied. "Your Uncle Joe starved ten million Ukrainians just to prove a point. So cut the charade. I wanted in on this stupid raid just to keep an eye on you, but oh, how the tables have turned. And the Russians get me as a bonus. So, to you and the KGB, I say, *na zdorovie*, comrades... *Na zdorovie*."

"Don't listen to this man!" McCreary said.

But Whitefeather and LaRoy stared at the deck, wracked with doubt.

DAY FOUR

Sept. 24, 1989
Camp Zhukov
Nome, Alaska

The Russians transferred the four men to another Hind sometime after midnight in Anchorage. At dawn, they found themselves flying over Nome. From above, McCreary could tell that the Russians had turned the town into a prison camp, wrapping it in a quadruple perimeter of fences. The entire sad spectacle was dusted with snow. Alexander had been dead wrong: the camp was full and getting fuller. As the Hind swooped in, McCreary could see dozens of shabbily dressed men staggering under guard from two rickety Ilyushin Il-18 turboprops, still bearing the Aeroflot logo along their spines. McCreary saw no other aircraft. Row upon row of barracks spread almost to the horizon, where thousands of men milled about. Alongside, like a cold blanket giving no comfort, lay the Bering Sea. The complex sat less than two hundred miles from the Soviet empire.

For the first time, McCreary saw Alexander sleeping. The spy's eyelids fluttered, half opened, and closed again as the chopper circled. McCreary jerked his thumb out the window and motioned to Whitefeather and LaRoy. The camp was real. And by definition, so must be the Superbridge.

"Wake him up!" he commanded to Whitefeather. The Indian slammed his shoulder into Alexander. The agent jolted awake.

"What do you see out the window, jackass?" McCreary said. "That sure is *some* KGB ops center." Alexander looked out the window and shrugged. Whitefeather shook his head. LaRoy sneered and looked out the window again. McCreary had his men back. Cold comfort, as the Hind settled down on the helipad. Two dozen Soviet soldiers greeted them. Once the hatches opened in this prison camp, God knew what waited.

The soldiers cut their bindings and marched them a quarter mile into the camp's parade ground. There, they found two hundred gaunt, bearded men, fresh off the turboprops. None in uniform. These men were slaves, harvested from the West Coast cities that the Russians had conquered. McCreary doubted the Russians needed the high guard towers that surrounded the parade ground. No roads led to Nome. It was nothing but permafrost and musk oxen for hundreds of miles. Besides, this was a broken bunch.

The men faced a stage, built in front of what looked like the prison's HQ. A long rank of Soviet officers in heavy coats and woolly hats lined the stage, regarding the American captives with disgust. McCreary counted ten red stars on ten woolly foreheads. To his surprise, McCreary also saw a woman, of all things, emerge from behind the officers.

She wore a gleaming white snowsuit, hugging her curves. Even the jacket barely concealed the shape of her narrow waist and high breasts. Topping all of it was a parka, lined in white fur that surrounded her delicate face. She stood next to a mountain of a Soviet officer, probably the camp commandant.

"Jeezum crow, look at her!" LaRoy whispered. "I thought they only make two kinds of Russian woman: fat and super-fat! But not that one!"

"That must be the commander's woman," Whitefeather said. "Gotta keep the boss warm, I reckon." Alexander smirked. On the stage, the giant colonel, with pockmarked skin and a huge gray mustache, stepped forward to the microphone.

"Defeated men of former U.S.A.: you have new home!" he said in a thick, guttural accent. "I am Colonel Boris Cherchenko of KGB. Organization, or escape will result in your death, and death of twenty comrades, which will select at random!" The Russian let this news sink in. McCreary looked around at the men around him. They weren't goin' anywhere. Skinny, dirty, and wearing scraggly beards—whether before or after the war had started, McCreary didn't know. You could never tell with the West Coast types. Their wide-eyed expressions betrayed fear at the sight of the Soviet officers—no, they were focused. Almost … *eager to help*. No wonder the Pacific states had rolled over on the first day of the war.

"And now," the Russian continued, "our camp commandant tells you more things!" He raised his fist with the rising cadence of his words, like Lenin on the back of a truck. "Listen if you wish to survive coming winter!"

McCreary expected one of the male officers to step forward. Instead, the woman stepped to the microphone, her boot heels rapping the plywood.

"I am Major General Valentina Vulvanova of the Soviet Far East Command," she said. Her accent was milder, almost cultured. The prisoners muttered. Their tone was appreciative. McCreary expected to hear murmurs similar to LaRoy's. Maybe these were real men, after all. But instead he heard words like "equality" and "advancement."

"Their leader is a woman!" one of them whispered to a fellow prisoner. *"Isn't that super?"*

"I knew I admired the Communists!"

"They got a little rough with our women in Berkeley, but they sure treat their own with respect!"

"You men," she said, "like hundreds of thousands of your countrymen in the compound behind you, are my guests."

A woman general? McCreary couldn't believe his eyes. But now that she'd stepped forward, her rank was plain as day: two gold stars each on either shoulder of her white snowsuit. It was said that the Soviets valued equality of the sexes, to the extreme of making their women fight in wars. McCreary wanted to shake his head in disgust— but he couldn't take his eyes off the woman onstage. "You will be a part of history," she was saying. "For the first time in twenty thousand years, Eurasia and North America will be linked. The finest socialist engineers will partner with you, the once proud American worker, to build humanity's greatest project. *The new Soviet-American Friendship Bridge shall end this foolish war!* And it will forever connect Mother Russia and the United Soviet States of America with an unbreakable bond."

McCreary shot Alexander a look. The spy said nothing, watching Vulvanova with a brutal glare.

"The work will be difficult," she said. "The bridge must be completed by spring if our glorious attempt to bring true freedom to America is to take place. Half of you will build a road from here to the city of Fairbanks. The rest will build the bridge. You shall weld and dig and hang from great heights. Most of you… will die. And when the man next to you expires, you shall replace him, propelled with a love of labor in your heart. You can cooperate—or we will build our bridge upon your frozen corpses."

McCreary whispered to Alexander, "Looks to me like they *are* building a bridge, you smug son of a bitch."

All around him, from the prisoners, McCreary caught more snippets, now terrified and uncertain:

"Socialism is about compassion! I don't understand! This seems so cruel!"

"A bridge across the Bering Strait? A road through the wilderness to Fairbanks? What about the environment, man?"

"They're asking me to build a bridge? I can't build anything. I'm a musician!"

This last man began to sob.

"Enough! Remember what my comrade told you," the woman general said. "The few of you who survive will be heroes of the Soviet-American Union! The rest…"

She cast one sidelong smirk at the bearded, unwashed bunch, and walked primly off the stage.

At that, the group was surrounded by AK-wielding Russians in snowsuits. They pushed through the crowd, gathering the men in groups of four or five. A few unwise souls asked questions—when the work would begin, where they would sleep, if vegetarian meals were available. One small man in wire-rimmed glasses claimed, in an effeminate voice, to be a professor of Marxist history. He asked if he could "sign a loyalty oath to the General

Secretary," whatever that was. The soldiers responded by beating the little man with gun butts, shattering his glasses, and his skull. The questions ceased, and the rest of the men moved, compliant.

McCreary turned to Whitefeather. "They're gonna split Alexander and me off. Get out of here no matter what and get word to the General. Don't wait for me! Git!"

Whitefeather had enough time to nod. Then, he and LaRoy were gone. As expected, Canadian Colonel Mortimer Tremblay reappeared and stepped between Alexander and McCreary. He grabbed McCreary and Alexander by the arm, and led them toward the stage.

"Our friends have a special reception for the both of you," Tremblay said, all smiles. They reached Vulvanova and the giant Soviet colonel, whereupon Tremblay saluted crisply. "General! It is an honour to see you again."

The woman ignored him and made eye contact with McCreary. Her steel blue eyes burned into him, so fierce that he blushed. "Colonel Tremblay, you have returned," Vulvanova said, still looking at McCreary. "These are the two men you were so excited to have captured, yes?"

"May I present Agent Robert Alexander of the CIA, and Major Michael McCreary of the United States Army. They were captured with two conscripts, who have been transferred to your labour division. As for these two, I'm sure your interrogators will be able to determine—"

"Colonel, why have you harmed this man?" Vulvanova's hand shot up to the side of McCreary's head. He felt her cool touch against the gash on his forehead.

"Your gallant Soviet grenadiers brought down their helicopter," Tremblay said. "Upon his capture, I must say that Major McCreary was … unforgivably rude."

Vulvanova shot the Canadian a glare. "Colonel, you may return to your outpost," she said. "If more American commandos come your way, please deal with them more elegantly." She turned to the Soviet colonel. "Boris, please take the American spy for processing." She examined McCreary's face up close. "Leave this one with me," she said. "I will interrogate him myself."

"But General—"

"That will be all, Colonel," Vulvanova said. She gave McCreary a ghost of a smile. McCreary felt an almost unfamiliar… urge. It had been so long since he'd lain with his wife. But regarding Vulvanova as anything other than the enemy was wrong. In so many ways! Besides, this was a trick. McCreary tried to summon Sunny's face as a defense, but he couldn't.

He glanced at Alexander as Tremblay grabbed the CIA man's elbow. Alexander's eyes were easy to read. *Just as I figured, McCreary.* At that, the giant Soviet colonel pushed Alexander toward the barracks. All McCreary could do was watch him go. If Alexander wanted to believe he'd set all this up, then so be it.

Then, McCreary felt the barrels of two AK-47s in his shoulders.

"Easy, comrades," Vulvanova said. "I need him in one piece." At first, McCreary wondered why she was giving the order in English, then realized it had been given for his benefit. *But why?* The Russian soldiers led McCreary toward a giant hangar complex past the fence. McCreary felt his treasonous eyes moving south along the general's body to her shapely behind. Walking became awkward and uncomfortable.

A light snow began to fall.

The soldiers led McCreary to a medic inside the hangar. For the next hour, the medic treated the cuts on his forehead and cheek, gave him a quick physical exam, then returned him to the guards. They put him into a windowless cell, and fed him a large breakfast: eggs, a tough cut of meat, and black bread. McCreary tried not to think about Whitefeather and LaRoy, shuttled off to a hellhole of a Soviet gulag.

Hours later the two guards returned and led him to a shower complex inside the hangar. His uniform— including the Medal of Honor—was taken away. He was given a stiff white towel and a hard bar of soap. To their credit, the guards let him shower in privacy behind an olive drab curtain. McCreary knew that Whitefeather and LaRoy hadn't had a hot shower in weeks, nor had the rest of the division back in Cheyenne. He did his best not to enjoy the hot spray, and to keep it brief.

He emerged from the shower to find the two guards standing next to a stool, upon which was stacked a pair of standard issue uniform pants, plus a white collared shirt. There were no shoes, boots, or even socks. McCreary toweled off and dressed himself. The flowing shirt had few buttons. When he tucked it in, much of his upper chest was exposed. This wasn't the kind of shirt a man should wear. Maybe a waiter from Europe, or California. The kinds of men they were massing outside, prepared to engineer the destruction of America with their soft, bare hands.

The general had set up her quarters toward the back of the hangar. Ornate stairs led above crates stamped in Cyrillic characters, to a balcony. It framed a pair of double doors—

French doors, McCreary had heard them called—hidden by curtains bathed in a soft glow from within. One of the soldiers at McCreary's side rapped on the doorframe and then snapped back. A doughy, bald man answered. He wore plain white clothes similar to McCreary's. There was something odd about the man. Something unthreatening. Like a steer. The soldiers shoved McCreary into the room. The man who had answered bowed, and backed away—leaving the room, closing the doors behind him.

The general's empty quarters were at once sparse, and ornate. They had been built into the hangar's Quonset, curved walls. Three tall, wood-framed windows at least ten feet tall had been cut into them. Gauzy curtains revealed little of the view beyond a hint of endless tundra. A sturdy fireplace gave off enough heat to make the room uncomfortably warm. No fewer than five polar bear rugs covered the floor. And dominating the far wall: a four-poster bed the size of a small swimming pool.

McCreary's bare feet had just hit the plush warmth of bear fur when Vulvanova emerged from her private washroom. Behind her, McCreary caught the hint of a brass mirror and a claw foot tub. But there was no time to appreciate the plumbing. Vulvanova barefoot, wearing a gold silk robe, covered in red Communist stars. Her thick, brunette curls were piled high on her head, trailing along her slender neck. McCreary wanted to look away—but as a man, he couldn't. The general padded up to him.

"Thank you for joining me, Major McCreary," she said. "May I call you Michael?"

"You may call me Michael J. McCreary," he stammered, "Major, United States Army, serial number 449—"

"As you wish," she said with a quick, delicate wave of her hand. "So stoic. But why are you blushing?"

71

"The shower. It was hot."

She shook her head. "Major McCreary, I was led to believe that you had seen a Soviet general up close before."

"Not one lookin' like you, I haven't."

"And what has brought you to Soviet Alaska?"

"You mean 'Alaska.' We're just curious about your bridge. Take some photos, get the T-shirt. I understand it will be quite a thing to see."

She smiled. "You should also see the three army groups we have across the water. If only your air force hadn't been so efficient against our transport capabilities before we got a foothold in America. If only your sailors had welcomed ours as comrades of the waves instead of the carnage that ensued. So, yes: a bridge. Long overdue." With that, Vulvanova sidled up to him. Her face was so close to his that he could feel her sweet, treacherous breath flowing from her perfect nose, onto his exposed collarbones.

With a sudden, silent snarl, she grabbed his shoulders—and ripped down the shirt. The few buttons popped and flew. McCreary didn't flinch. Vulvanova stood back to admire his torso, framed in the ruined shirt that hung from his waistband and constrained his arms. He stood still and tried to control his breathing as she walked around him, now and then trailing a delicate finger along his lower stomach, hips, and waist.

"As I'm sure you imagine, Major, I am a woman of certain… appetites," she said. She peeled the shirt from his waistband, freeing his arms. "I am a direct descendant of Catherine the Great. Do you know your Russian rulers?"

McCreary remembered something about a Russian queen of loose morals. Heard tell, her habits got so out of control that she'd died under the weight of a horse. "I'm just a humble Texas boy, General," he said. "I never paid much attention in history class."

"Just as well. But you must understand that I have found it lonely in this barren wilderness."

"The bridge—" he said.

"Oh, Major," she purred, her lips near his ear. "Must we discuss this terrible war? I've learned that making love to American men is much more satisfying than fighting them."

"Is that what this camp is for?" he asked. "Gatherin' up as many boyfriends as you can?"

Vulvanova moved in front of him, wrists balanced on his shoulders. "We have captured an abundance of weak, educated males from your most decadent West Coast cities. Professors. Artists. Intellectuals from… *San Francisco*." She sounded disgusted. "None of them able to perform in the presence of a strong, fertile Russian woman!"

At that, she reached behind her head and pulled a long ivory pin. Her hair dropped like an avalanche of dark silk around her shoulders. She tossed the pin into a corner, loosened the belt of her robe, and let the garment fall around her ankles in a soft, Communist puddle. It took all of McCreary's resolve to stare not at her body, but into those steely blue eyes.

Vulvanova's wrists found their way around his shoulders again. He felt a pair of soft points grazing his bare chest. "Your wife," she whispered against his lips. "Even after she became a good Russian girl, she refused to give you her heart. Or her body."

"How many armored divisions—?"

"This Russian woman will not make the same mistake."

73

With that, Vulvanova planted an open-mouthed kiss on McCreary's lips. His resistance melted.

He had tried to be true... true to what? He thought of Alexander, probably having his own intimate moment with a cattle prod and a circular saw. He felt no guilt. To hell with him.

"Major McCreary," Vulvanova breathed when she broke the kiss. "Michael—tonight, you are not an American soldier. I am not a Soviet general. We are man and woman. And outside, it snows."

They kissed again. Valentina Vulvanova pressed her supple Slavic flesh against his, McCreary surrendered to the Soviet general—and seized her!

Hours of lovemaking followed. Throughout, a series of exotic Russian sexual methods and positions whose names Vulvanova purred in the darkness: Laika the Space Dog... Plowing the Collective... Onion-Doming... Diverting the Volga... Moose and Squirrel...

"And this one is called... *Breaking the Siege of Stalingrad*," she moaned expertly. Sunny had satisfied McCreary as a wife, but... praise be unto Mother Russia. Midway through their frenetic seventh session, Vulvanova began babbling in Russian, and when McCreary had ordered her to address him in English, she cried out, "God bless America!" and "Lenin's mother was a whore!"

And at her seventh or eighth climax, the most satisfying: *"I spit on the worker's revolution!"*

Vulvanova was an open, passionate book—and that book's pages were petal-soft. With every twitching, pulsing climax, Vulvanova told McCreary a little more. Toward the end of the night, McCreary had assembled a decent strategic map of the Soviet Far East. He asked her about troop movements. Spring offensives. *Strategic thrusts.* As orgasm after orgasm coursed through the general's body—and his own—McCreary realized once more that the outlook for America wasn't good.

The Russians were *coming*, indeed.

Before the last session—their tenth of the night—Vulvanova got out of bed and slinked her naked way across a polar bear skin, toward a lacquer box. McCreary watched her body in amazement. She returned, climbed aboard the bed, and returned the Medal of Honor around McCreary's neck. "You shall be my war husband," she said, "and you will never know sadness again."

The general lay on her side, like a model in those European paintings from the old days. She turned her back to McCreary, looked at him over her shoulder in the flickering firelight, and purred, "Make love to me like the great American hero that you are."

McCreary complied. His last memory before spiraling off into their sad, traitorous ecstasy was the Medal of Honor around his taut neck, as it swayed, and swayed, and swayed…

DAY FIVE

Sept. 25, 1989
Camp Zhukov

McCreary awoke to the two guards from the day before standing at the foot of Vulvanova's bed, AKs pointing at him. He reached sideways and found the General's side of the bed empty. It was then he heard running water flowing into a bathtub.

McCreary sat up, aching from his injuries and not much sleep. He felt the Medal of Honor's cold, heavy tap against his collarbone. He knew better than to call for Vulvanova's help. She was finished with him. This wasn't her first rodeo. He should be grateful for the intel, and hope that Vlad and Igor here didn't riddle him with 7.62x39mm rounds before he could share it.

McCreary pulled on his pants, both legs at once. "Does this place have room service?"

They dumped him, hands bound, in front of a long barracks hall. The two guards drove away in their jeep, parting a sad group of staggering prisoners along the way. A light flurry of pellet snow sprinkled the frozen mud around his head. McCreary felt two strong arms pull him up by his shoulders and drag him to the barracks door.

"Welcome home, Major," Whitefeather said from his left.

"Boy, have we got a story to tell you," LaRoy said from his right.

They whisked him inside. The barracks air was dark, fetid, and barely warmer than outside. Unshaven men stared at him from between rows of bunk beds. The sergeants guided McCreary down the length of the barracks and set him next to a single, ineffectual wood stove. McCreary sat on a small stool, while Whitefeather cut the zipties around his wrists with a makeshift knife made from a piece of bone and a green bottle shard. Pure Whitefeather.

"You don't look that worse for wear," LaRoy said. "What'd they do to you last night, Major?"

McCreary massaged his wrists, and looked at the splintered floor. "Don't worry about me. Looks like you two had it worse." He looked past his men down the long, grim hall. At least a hundred filthy men lounged, dangled their legs, and played card games on the floor. They smelled like they looked. The men also seemed wary. Afraid. To their credit, the men had made their bunks. Neat, from the looks of things. At least they weren't completely worthless.

"What about Alexander?" McCreary asked.

Whitefeather shook his head. "We saw the Russians take him into town. When men go into Nome proper, they don't come back. That's the word on the street."

"I spent the night with that Soviet general," McCreary said. "Less said the better. But she gave me good … intel. Let's just hope I can trust it." He tried to be dismissive, but as he sat and stared into the shadows, he recalled the steamy night. His face flushed. LaRoy and Whitefeather exchanged a look. "She says they've got three army groups across the strait, just like Pearce said," McCreary went on. "But I don't get it: if they got a Superbridge in the works, how come these men are loungin' around?"

LaRoy hunkered down and rubbed his hands. "Hear that wind out there, Major? They've only got two planes to run their engineering staff back and forth. Planes are taking off and landing around the clock. Once the weather lifts, these men say they expect to start work. This group of barracks is called the Lenin Brigade—they're building the road to Fairbanks. The Stalins are in the complex over yonder. They're the hardier bunch. They'll build the bridge. The Russians have a camp like this one on the other side, with a bunch of British and French fellas. Hear tell, the Eurotrash fell in with Ivan quicker than our'n."

Yeah, but that was a bunch of Europeans. McCreary stood and looked at the filthy group before him. "A more pathetic bunch I never did see. How could these yahoos build a damn thing?"

"That's not my problem," Whitefeather said. "But this might be." He kicked aside a foul-smelling wool blanket that had been tossed into a corner. The blanket had been hiding a trapdoor, barely visible in the gloom. Whitefeather yanked up the hatch—his forearms bulged under his long, greasy sleeves, as the damn thing looked like it weighed eighty pounds. McCreary looked over his shoulders at the loafing, lounging bunch, and decided it didn't matter if they saw.

"Go in," Whitefeather said, "have a look-see."

The air from the dark, square opening was frigid. McCreary already could see his breath. "It must be twenty below down there," he said.

"This building looks like it was an old warehouse," Whitefeather replied. "Whoever built it cut a basement out of permafrost. The Russians must not have searched the place very well before they threw men in here."

"What's down there?" McCreary asked. Whitefeather responded by handing the major his Zippo. "See for yourself, sir," Whitefeather said, "but do Alaska a favor, and don't drop that."

McCreary took the lighter, fell to his stomach, and flicked the flame. His eyes adjusted, and he gasped. Whitefeather was right about the permafrost; the nearby walls gleamed dirty white in the Zippo's glow. But it was the next thing McCreary noticed that made him draw in his breath. The basement reached as long and as wide as the barracks itself. Neat rows of crate after crate, covered in gleaming frost, stretching into black. Each was the size of a steamer trunk. The closest, to the right of the trapdoor, made its contents clear in bright red letters:

HIGH EXPLOSIVES
LEND-LEASE SHIPMENT
NO SMOKING
BY ORDER OF THE WAR DEPARTMENT
AND PRESIDENT ROOSEVELT, F.D.
PROPERTY OF U.S.S.R. (C.C.C.P.)

"I'll be a son of a gun," McCreary whispered. He sat up, swung his feet around, and dropped into the hole.

The ceiling was low, six feet above the dirt floor. McCreary stepped along at a crouch, the Zippo's faint glow illuminating a bare fragment of what the room had to offer. A crate of M-1 rifles, its lid half open. Another box, this one filled with M1905 bayonets. Boxes and boxes of ammunition.

There were a few odd items—McCreary found himself staring at a disassembled PA system, plus a record player with an LP of Jazz Age patriotic tunes.

How had the Russians missed all this? Crates of cold-weather gear. Guns. Ammunition. Machinery.

Machinery! McCreary thought. *The machinery of God, is more like it!*

A few moments later, he handed the Zippo back to Whitefeather, who hauled him out of the basement with one hand.

"My great-granddad got drafted off the rez and came up here to ship weapons to the Russians during the Second World War," Whitefeather was saying. "Looks like the Army forgot to ship the leftovers home. Then, someone forgot they forgot."

"Looks like the Russians forgot a thing or two, as well," McCreary said. "You're welcome for the help, comrades."

Whitefeather nodded. "If it hadn't been for us, they'd all be speakin' German."

"What were we shippin' 'em?"

"One crate of C3 and about twenty tons of everything else."

Whitefeather replaced the trapdoor and kicked the blanket over it. McCreary looked at the miserable, slothful tide in the barracks and shook his head. The cache in the basement felt like a cruel joke. Below his feet lay everything he needed to take down this camp. But counting himself, there were only three qualified, Free World marksmen within five hundred miles.

What had happened to the Home of the Brave, anyway? Where had things gone so wrong? "And here we are stuck with this bunch," he muttered to Whitefeather. "I've never been more ashamed to be an

American." He spat on the floor. But the big Indian gave another sly grin.

LaRoy had heard him, too. "Oh, yeah?" LaRoy said. "Watch this." The wiry West Virginian stood straight, pulled down the front of his jacket, puffed out his chest, and strode down the main aisle. "You cowardly bunch of maggots!" he yelled. *FALL IN!*"

There came a sudden cacophony of feet—loafers and dress shoes and moccasins—thumping to the floor as the men piled out of their bunks. They created two parallel columns that lined the aisle. LaRoy walked down the middle, hands behind his back.

Whitefeather leaned down and whispered, "Sir, you never shoulda made him a sergeant."

LaRoy hollered at the men. His voice was hidden from the Russian guardtowers only by the howling Bering Sea gale that now lashed the barracks. "You miserable pudknockers! That's your new C.O., Major Michael McCreary, winner of the Medal of Honor! He was goin' toe-to-toe with Ivan when you ballerinas were welcomin' the Russians down Main Street with hoochie-cooch and handjobs! You make me sick!" LaRoy reached the barracks door then spun back around. He strode back toward a slender young man. The kid wore a thick cable knit sweater and torn white jeans. He had a shock of blond hair sweeping across his forehead. The kid flinched but kept his erect posture as LaRoy stopped in front of him, two inches from his chest. "YOU! Catcher in the Rye! I just bet you love to curl up with a good book and a cup of herbal tea! Where you from, college boy?"

"Sir! Sonoma County, California, sir!"

LaRoy jerked his head back. "Sonoma County?! What do you do in Sonoma County—besides sip cocktails in your pixie castle with your pinky in the air?!"

"Sir! My family owned a vineyard before the Russians turned it into a potato farm, sir!"

"The goddamn Commies did you a favor! What kind of girly-man owns a vineyard? Did you make *RO-SAY* in your vineyard, you maggot?"

"Sir! Rosé is an inferior blend, sir! My family made pinot grigios and chardonnays, sir!"

LaRoy's voice rose in disbelief. "Shar-duh—*WHAT*? Did you correct me, you little wine-sipping, cheese-eating, bubblebath-taking FAIRY?"

The kid's face quivered. "Sir! No sir! I just wanna kill Russians, sir!"

"Not with that New Wave-o haircut you won't! Drop and give me twenty!"

The kid from Marin County did as he was told. The young man fell to the floor and did some wobbly pushups at LaRoy's feet. But the sergeant already had moved on and wasn't critiquing his form.

For the better part of fifteen minutes, LaRoy badgered and insulted the men—a musician from Portland, an artisan cheese maker from Seattle, the inevitable choreographer from San Francisco, each more delicate than the last. But on their faces, McCreary saw nothing but the flickering fire of determination. "I don't believe it!" McCreary marveled. "You boys turned them from yellow-bellied sympathizers into real men! These fellas could die for their country tomorrow!"

"Major," Whitefeather deadpanned as the LaRoy show went on, "you weren't the only one who didn't get any sleep last night."

But breaking out of the camp would take more than LaRoy carryin' on. "What're we supposed to do with 'em?" McCreary asked.

"That's your job, sir," Whitefeather whispered. "Now, watch this: LaRoy's about to give the final exam."

"You!" LaRoy was shouting at a short Hispanic man with a blue bandana around his head. "Get that rag off your dome, you gang-bangin', drugstore-robbin' meatstick! Are you from East L.A., Pablo? I bet you drive an Impala with the Virgin Mary painted on the hood!"

"Sir! *María Madre de Dios adorna el toldo de mi El Camino!* I represent Oakland, sir! Name's Sanchez, sir!"

"What's the greatest country on God's green earth, Private Sanchez?"

"Sir! The United States of America, sir!"

LaRoy's voice pitched up an enraged octave. He screamed in Sanchez's face: *"But I thought the United States of America is a terrorist nation of imperialism, and the Russians are our friends!"*

"Sir, the Communists are raping, pillaging Mongols!" Sanchez called back. "Bent on destroying freedom, corrupting our women, and smashing private enterprise, sir!"

LaRoy smiled. "At ease, men!" With a muffled thump, their right feet shifted, arms locked behind them. LaRoy turned and faced McCreary. He stood at attention. "Major McCreary!" he called out. "I present to you the newest bunch of volunteers in the U.S. Army! They ain't much to look at, but they're ready to do their part for God and country, sir!"

Above the howling wind, McCreary swore he could hear the swelling of violins. He bowed his head. The weary son of Texas wiped away a tear and felt the itch of a plan coming together. "So, Major," Whitefeather said, "it'll be dark in a couple hours. What kind of mischief are we gonna make?"

DAY SIX

Sept. 26, 1989
Camp Zhukov

The weather lifted after midnight. The storm had dumped six inches of wispy white powder all over the camp. Three hours later, wearing cold weather gear from the basement treasure-trove, his face blackened, McCreary raised the heavy, World War II–era M-3 binoculars and studied the barracks. Those brave, doomed men! Such was the worst part of war, that you could mold men into warriors, only to know that the gods would smash them to bits.

McCreary felt it—the fatigue, the need for hot food and a warm bed. The sweet treachery of Valentina Vulvanova's smooth skin. These were the things he wanted more than anything. Some undisciplined part of his mind told him that having those things meant that the fighting was done.

As McCreary watched the barracks, three Russian sentries strolled in front of the front door, AKs slung over their shoulder. Twin spotlights danced to their right in lazy patterns. Behind the barracks complex, McCreary

85

studied the five guard towers, each armed with PK machine guns and a pair of shivering Ivans.

He swung the binoculars to his right. A hundred yards farther down, LaRoy and Whitefeather prepped the fence with the other surprise they'd found in the basement. McCreary tried to keep his rattled nerves under control as he waited for their signal.

On the runway, McCreary could see and hear one of the Il-18s revving its engines. A plane: that was the prize. McCreary remembered enough basic flight training to get the bird off the ground. Landing the crate might be another matter. But their targets were sixty Soviet divisions across the strait. A safe landing wasn't their biggest problem.

Hidden in the snow next to him lay the body of the Soviet sentry whose throat McCreary had cut. McCreary shouldered the man's AK, tucked himself into the pump house's shadows, and took another look.

Far in the distance, he spotted the main hangar complex. There were the triple windows to General Vulvanova's quarters, hidden by the gauze curtains. Her lights were on. *What could she be doing at this hour?*

As if in response, the general raised her delicate head and unmistakable brunette curls into view. McCreary increased his magnification—and saw more than he wanted. The foot of Vulvanova's bed. A muscular, hairy leg, toes flexing. And Vulvanova, wearing her red silk robe, wiping the corner of her mouth with the back of her hand. She had just completed a sex act.

McCreary felt an unwelcome burning in his chest. Jealousy! He had done his best to set aside the memories of the night before, and concentrate on the mission. But there she was. Vulvanova… *Valentina*… with another man? And who was he? She and McCreary couldn't have just spent hours intertwined—and then have the night mean *nothing*. Seducing and conquering was the prerogative of men.

Was this what Communism did to a woman's virtue?

McCreary couldn't pull his eyes away. Vulvanova crawled like a cat up the man's body. The last thing he saw were her slender calves, her delicate feet, sliding along the man's legs in a slow, familiar dance of afterglow.

I'm so sorry, Sunny. Guess I got what I deserved.

McCreary swung the binoculars to the right. The turboprop ran its engines, sitting on the frozen tarmac. And then, so faint he almost missed it, the flicker of Whitefeather's Zippo.

Once.

Twice.

McCreary picked up a light switch, attached to a wire that ran back to the barracks. He said a silent prayer, and flicked it on.

At first, McCreary heard nothing but the sleeping camp. The plan had failed. The wire running under the snow was too long, or it had come loose.

But then, McCreary heard the distinct sound of trumpets from the PA speakers he'd mounted behind the barracks' shuttered windows. A few bars later came the bright, brassy tones of a curvy torchlight singer, clear as a bell even a football field away:

"O Beautiful…

"For spacious skies…"

McCreary checked the AK-47's clip for the third time.

The Russians did what Mike McCreary hoped they would the second they heard the music: they rushed the building and demanded entry, banging on the door and splintering it with their rifle butts. The bonus was the huge Soviet colonel who had greeted them their first day in camp. McCreary watched man stagger about the parade grounds drunk, bellowing at his subordinates. Two seconds after LaRoy and Whitefeather blew the det-cord—and with it four layers of fence leading to the airstrip—McCreary threw the second switch.

He tried to brace himself and drop his head into the snow. Even that simple motion took too long. Twenty pounds of vintage C3 sent out a blast wave at twenty-five thousand feet per second, faster than men had traveled to the moon. The explosion lifted McCreary and the dead sentry like scarecrows and threw them into the side of the pumphouse, which collapsed under their weight. As McCreary landed, he saw the mushroom cloud from the barracks rise into the air above him, a churning ball of flame that turned night into day.

Then rained the debris. A splintered two-by-four streaked in and impaled the dead sentry two feet from McCreary. The lid to the woodstove crashed into the remains of the pump house to his right. A bloody arm landed in the snow. At one end, the splintered ends of forearm bone; at the other, an accusatory finger, pointed at McCreary. Etched across the wrinkled skin of the hand, the tattoo of an NKVD dagger.

McCreary pushed himself to his feet. More debris fell around him—spinning plywood, a delicately flaming blanket, a leg. He became aware of the first Russian sentries running in his direction toward the explosion. In the faint glow of the compound lights, their snowsuits looked like ghosts gliding through the darkness. LaRoy and Whitefeather's det-cord had created a giant gap in the fences, and beyond it, the Aeroflot's propellers spun on the tarmac.

Six, no, seven of the soldiers ran toward the ruined barracks—and McCreary. He lurched forward, grabbed the sentry's AK-47, and stepped out of the shadows.

The lead man spotted him first and brought his rifle up, twenty feet away. McCreary cut him in half. Killing the rest was easy. By the time the last man fell, only one of them had managed to get off a single errant shot. McCreary finished off one screaming, dying guard with a bullet to the head. Then he turned and watched the battle unfold.

Five of LaRoy's prisoner-soldiers had thrown off their snowy blankets and rushed the nearest guard tower. One of them, a slender kid in wire frame glasses and a set of fatigues two sizes too big, raised his vintage M-1 carbine and squeezed off shots. It was the first firearm he'd ever fired, but one connected and sent a guard tumbling to the ground. His buddy, a comparative lit professor from Eugene, lit the fuse on one of Whitefeather's pipe bombs. The little man put his right foot forward and tossed the bomb with his delicate right wrist. It landed far short, of course, but by the time it blew the fence apart, his friend, a pale writer by the name of Wesley Featherton, lobbed his pipe bomb true. Miraculously, it landed next to the still surprised machine gunner and turned the entire tower into a splintery fireball. The gunner sailed toward the ground, screaming, on fire.

Meanwhile, Private Sanchez's crew rushed the main gate station, just as Whitefeather had instructed. Blasting away with their M-1s, they created enough confusion that Sanchez had time to throw two bombs into the building. They detonated and took a half-dozen Ivans with them.

By the time Whitefeather yelled McCreary's name from the tarmac, all eight dozen of LaRoy's platoon had spread across the camp. They unloaded their M-1s into unsuspecting sentries, blew up guard towers, and tossed weapons to their surprised fellow prisoners emerging from the other barracks. But it wasn't Whitefeather that got McCreary running. It was the sight of the blond kid, the one from Marin County that LaRoy had first dressed down. The brave young man, the son of a winemaker, led a valiant charge on a corner guard tower. He turned to order his men forward, one arm holding his rifle, the other urging his men into the fight. The Soviet machine gunner in the tower heard him, and brought his PK around.

McCreary couldn't watch. He turned and heard the burst from the PK as he reached the fence.

McCreary cleared the coiled wire and charged across the tarmac. Ahead of him, the Ilyushin started a slow roll forward, its side hatch hanging open. Whitefeather clambered aboard, turning in the doorway and beckoning fiercely. "Hurry, Major!" he thundered above the engines. "Don't turn around! Don't look back!"

What could Whitefeather could be talking about? Of course he wouldn't turn around. What would he see, anyway, besides a doomed fight that he desperately wanted to join?

Then he heard the squealing brakes.

"Michael! Stop!"

McCreary stopped running, and turned.

Valentina Vulvanova sat a few yards away behind the wheel of her jeep. Extended in her white-gloved hand, the beautiful Soviet general held a small, silver automatic. It trembled.

"Don't make me shoot!" she said. "You were to stay here with me!"

"Your men didn't get the memo," he called back. "They trussed me up like a turkey and dumped me with the trash."

"Major!" Whitefeather yelled. "We have to hit the trail!"

"It was a mistake!" Tears streamed down Vulvanova's face. "I won't permit you to leave!" When McCreary backed away toward the plane, she pleaded: "When you made your plans for escape… why didn't you come for me?"

"You had company, General," he said.

"He meant nothing to me!" she said. "It was only to forget you!"

"Sorry, darlin'," he said. "I got a plane to catch." But he couldn't bring himself to turn away.

"I'll shoot you rather than let you go!" she cried.

Gunshot.

McCreary flinched and put his hand to his chest—only to pull it away, clean.

Twenty feet away, a red star blossomed on the front of Vulvanova's snowsuit. Her eyes wide, her mouth open in a silent call of alarm, she slumped sideways and fell out of the idling jeep into the snow.

McCreary turned around, horrified that his proud warrior would ever gun down a woman. But Whitefeather had been replaced. Meeting his gaze were the bruised, expressionless eyes of Robert Alexander. One hand braced the hatch's upper edge, the other held a semi-automatic pistol.

"Let's go, McCreary!" Alexander yelled. "If you can fly a plane, now's the time!"

McCreary turned and ran to Vulvanova. She had fallen at an unnatural angle and hit the tarmac hard. The fringe of her hood glowed white in the airstrip lights like a halo. Her beautiful blue eyes were losing their focus.

"Michael," she whispered. "There is so much… to tell you…"

He picked her up in his arms. "Stay with me, Valentina," he said. "You're gonna be fine."

"No!" she rasped. "The bridge. Our ambitious dream… so wasteful." Then she coughed. A spray of blood landed on the shoulders of her snowsuit.

"Remember me," she whispered, and died in his arms.

Alexander, behind him: *"McCREARY!"*

At that, Major Michael McCreary kissed the dead Soviet general on her forehead and lowered her onto the tarmac. "*Do svidanya*, Valentina." Her funeral song would be the sounds of explosions, gunshots, and the screams of the dying. He closed Valentina's eyes, shouldered his AK, and sprinted toward the taxiing plane.

The first thing McCreary did when he pulled himself into the plane was pull the door shut. The second was to stow his AK-47. The third was to sock Bob Alexander in the jaw.

The spy grunted and tumbled back between the seats. McCreary didn't bother to see if he got up. He had a plane to fly. He turned toward the cockpit to find the instrument panel and windshield splattered with bone, blood, and brains.

LaRoy pulled the headless pilot out of the left seat. It was then that McCreary noticed the dead copilot outside the cockpit door.

"It was Alexander, sir," LaRoy said. "Whitefeather and I commandeered this plane and found Alexander tied up in the back. They were going to fly him to Anchorage for questioning. The minute we freed him, he shot these two point blank."

"We kill because we have to," McCreary said. "He just likes killin'."

But there was no time to talk about it. A pair of explosions shook the plane. McCreary wedged into the pilot seat and fought his panic: he couldn't fly this bird. All of the dials and gauges were in Russian, and for every one that looked like it performed some familiar function, it was in the wrong place. That left McCreary little else to do but point the Ilyushin toward the longest airstrip, lean on the throttles, and pull back on the stick for all it was worth.

06:15
An Ilyushin Il-18
Bering Strait

The ride was bumpy as McCreary flew out over the icy water, the headwinds picking up. Keeping his heading due west taxed his nascent skill. Before making landfall on the Asian mainland, the plane entered a cloudbank. McCreary felt his rusty instrumentation skills coming back. He needn't have panicked. The Russian bird wasn't that dissimilar from the planes he'd flown at the Academy. It was heavier, slower. The Russians had forged it from frying pans.

McCreary had ordered LaRoy and Whitefeather to raid the galley and get some sleep. Neither man had enjoyed a nap or a meal in days. As the rising sun stabbed gaps in the clouds with spears of gold, Alexander worked his way into the cockpit and sat in the copilot's seat.

"How's your jaw?" McCreary asked.

"How about I just say 'You're welcome'?" Alexander asked. "You know, I could have warned you about Vulvanova. Men don't send stable women to Alaska." McCreary glanced at him sidelong, hoping to see a bruise from his right cross. But the Russians had worked the spy over good. Alexander's movie-star looks had seen better days.

"*You* should be thanking *us*," McCreary said.

Alexander snorted, and wiped the pilot's blood from the altimeter. "All your men did was complicate things. And that mess you made while you were escaping: the Russians *wish* they could kill as many Americans as you have today!"

"Those men died with a purpose," McCreary said. "We gave them something to fight for." He smiled. With one punch, Alexander had lost whatever power over him that he'd once held. The major was more worried about the low fuel gauge.

"Turn this plane around, McCreary," Alexander said. "I've built my career on brains and luck. And the second has run out. I want to go *home*. I want to live!"

"I want my *country* to live," McCreary said.

"What about Whitefeather and LaRoy? Are you going to get them killed, too?"

"They knew what they were gettin' into."

"There is nothing over here but taiga and death. If you're looking for proof for General Pearce, you won't find it. There will be no army groups. All of this was a ruse. I still believe that. "

And at that moment, the Il-18 emerged from the clouds. They now flew a mere five hundred feet above the largest assembly of military hardware either man had ever seen, and likely would ever see again.

Spread in neat diagonal rows below them were tanks and trucks and APCs. Thousands of them. Tens of thousands. The Russians had parked so much armor on the barren Siberian plain that it reminded McCreary of driving through the Kansas cropland in springtime. The vehicles whizzed below them in dizzying patterns of alternating gray, tan, and white. Off along the horizon, across a wide, silver river sidewinding into the ocean, lay a town much like Nome. Only this time, the long, straight barracks that the Russians had added stretched past the edges of the earth.

"Oh, looky here," McCreary said. "What are those down there, Mr. Alexander? T-72s? T-80s?" He turned and looked at Alexander. "You tell me. You're the expert, ain't you?"

"That's Provideniya," Alexander breathed out. "They've turned it into a base. My god. You were right all along. I've been such a fool. McCreary—get us out of here."

"Don't you worry your pretty little head," McCreary said. He was already banking the Ilyushin to the right in some vain hope that they hadn't been spotted, and if so, that no one on this side of the strait had heard tell of goings on across the water.

Alexander's hand fell on McCreary's shoulder, his head shaking as he took in square mile after square mile of Soviet military might. "Oh, god, McCreary, I'm so sorry, I'm so sorry."

"There's no time for that!" McCreary snapped. He shook Alexander's hand off his shoulder just as the low fuel alarm sounded. "I'm going to have to set this thing down. Start rustlin' around those charts over by the navigator table. Find us a road north away from this mess, close to something with a transmitter."

Alexander stared at him. "Certainly you don't mean we're going to land *here.*"

"There's a MiG base outside of Anchorage. If we try to head back east, we're done for. Besides: we need to find a radio. Now."

"We won't last two days on this side of the Strait!"

"This was a one-way trip and you knew it," McCreary said. "Follow my order, or I'll have Whitefeather scalp you and throw you out the side."

Alexander climbed out of the copilot's chair and combed through the charts.

Alexander found them a straight, wide gravel road that parted an endless sea of anemic pines. The Ilyushin had been designed for just such a landing, but McCreary didn't trust his skills enough to use the flaps without stalling. He brought them in screaming hot. The rear gear came in okay, but when the nose touched down, it dug into the gravel like a plow and collapsed. The plane spun right, McCreary overcorrected, and the entire thing careened left, off the road, into the trees. A horrible symphony of grinding, disintegrating metal erupted from the port-side wing as the engines shook themselves apart. The plane came to rest on its side at a forty-five degree angle.

No fire. Yet.

McCreary undid his harness and looked over at Alexander. At first, he thought the man was dead. His windows were cracked, and the instruments on that side of the plane smoked. But the spy lifted his head, looked at McCreary, and said, "Well, we're on the ground. We have an hour to live."

McCreary pushed himself out of the seat. He stepped over the tangled bodies of the flight crew, one embracing the other in death like lovers. In the cabin, he found Whitefeather and LaRoy unhooking their seatbelts, craning their heads around, looking through the chaos for their gear.

"Fine landing, Major," LaRoy said without any trace of humor. "What next?"

God, he loved his men.

The march began. McCreary put Lonestar in basic fire team formation. Among the toys Whitefeather had found in Nome was a Browning machine gun. He walked at the rear, belts of ammunition draped across his chest like a necklace of dinosaur teeth. McCreary put LaRoy to the left, himself as fire team leader to the right, and Alexander on point.

A half-mile behind them and receding lay the wreckage of the Il-18. Alexander was right: they had maybe an hour before someone spotted the lazy cone of smoke and wiped them out.

Each man, doomed as he was—exposed and striding down the road—scanned the trees nervously.

"Three AK-47s and a Browning M1919A6 made in Utah," LaRoy said round the first bend. "A sorrier outfit I never did see."

"This road can't be much more than three months old," McCreary said watching his feet sink into two inches of gravel. "I'll bet it leads to Cape Dezhnev. Perfect staging road for a bridge and everything it's designed to carry."

"How far to the station?" Whitefeather asked.

"Eight miles, maybe less," Alexander said. His head darted back and forth, looking for the Russian ambush that, had it been waiting, would have killed them ten minutes before. The CIA man was terrified. He was no longer in control.

Worst of all, he knew he was no longer *right.* McCreary studied the back of his head with grim satisfaction.

"Hey, Charlie," LaRoy asked his Indian friend, "what're the spirit winds tellin' ya?"

"Nothin'," Whitefeather said. "Nothin' at all."

McCreary laughed, bitterly. "How can that be, Sergeant? We're thirty klicks away from half the Soviet Army! I'd a thought you'd smell the leather in their boots."

"I reckon I'm a little too far from home is all," Whitefeather said, quiet and wistful. "Or maybe we're about to die and the spirit winds have died with us. Either way."

McCreary nodded. What could he say to such wisdom?

The station showed itself an hour before they reached it. Antennae, slender and fat, simple or studded with drum-like microwave transmitters, did a poor impression of the trees that surrounded them. Whitefeather and LaRoy broke left, and McCreary took Alexander with him to the right. Instinct took over and he sprinted, hunched over low, through the wide spaces in the trees. It felt good to run. And if Alexander couldn't keep up, he could just miss all the fun, thank you very much.

But when McCreary reached the edge of the station, and dove forward behind some tangled brush, Alexander flopped on his belly right beside him. A generator thudded somewhere. "What now?" Alexander hissed. The spy's anger and bitterness had returned.

It was plain to see why. Twenty yards ahead, three T-72s were parked next to the small cinderblock station, engines off. Through the front window, a young Russian officer studied a sheaf of papers, then glanced at a bank of radio dials.

"No sign of the crews," McCreary said.

"They're not here."

"Inside the tanks, maybe?"

"Nothing more unpleasant to sleep in than a T-72. They're storing them here."

"Why?"

"I don't know," Alexander said. "But that man's alone."

"You'd better be right."

Alexander steadied his rifle. "I can hit him from here. One shot."

"No," McCreary said. "If you miss, you'll hit the radio. Besides: I've seen enough brain matter for one day."

McCreary looked to his left, hearing a birdcall. Whitefeather. "You stay here," McCreary whispered. He sprinted low to the right without waiting for an answer. He hit the ground in time to see LaRoy land on his belly next to the innermost T-72. An instant later, a spray of pebbles from Whitefeather clattered against the front window. They were going to capture him alive. Good men.

Inside, the young officer stood straight, startled. He set the papers down, peered through the window sideways. He held a thick, white coffee mug. The door opened, and the young man, the creases on his crisp uniform apparent even from where McCreary spied, stepped outside. Inches from the tank. Inches from LaRoy.

"*Vladimir?*" the officer called into the trees. "*Mischa? Pavel? Ostanovit' vozit'sya—*"

His head disappeared in a red spray against the side of the building. The young officer slumped against the cinderblock, spilling his coffee against the front of his uniform. It was then that McCreary noticed echoes from the single shot. They rolled through the trees, and wouldn't stop, no matter how much McCreary prayed they would. "Damn you, Alexander!"

McCreary shot to his feet as LaRoy staggered to his. Whitefeather emerged a moment later. Finally, Alexander trotted alongside one of the tanks, barrel of his AK-47 smoking. Whitefeather studied the dead man at his feet. He shook his head. It was getting to him, too. A single tear rolled down his face.

"Too much killin'," he said.

McCreary snatched the rifle from Alexander. "That's it," he said. "You're done. You get in there and dial the frequency I tell you. Get General Pearce on the horn. Then you're on your own."

Alexander turned and entered the station. "Have it your way, slugger," he said. McCreary handed the spy's rifle to LaRoy, stepped over the dead officer, and followed Alexander into the station.

"Once more, son, just so I know!" said Pearce's faint, faraway voice.

"Ivan's throwin' snowballs!" McCreary shouted into the mic, pressing the headset against his ear. "Take the family to the ballpark!"

Alexander pulled open file cabinets, scanning sheaves of documents. When he finished a page, often in less than five seconds, he threw it over his shoulder. Ever the spy. Outside the building, LaRoy crouched next to the innermost T-72. He had an AK in either hand, regarding the surrounding pines with, at best, casual interest. Whitefeather stood in the open a few yards closer to the trees, Browning dipped. Both men knew that the fight was over, one way or another. Maybe they had twenty minutes left. Maybe two. The Soviet Army would be coming, dressed to the nines. Even if Lonestar somehow evaded capture, winter was coming. And it was a long walk home.

"*God bless!*" the general replied over a faint whine. "*It's a great day for a ballgame!*"

"Roger that, sir! The skiin' in the mountains ain't so good! Repeat: the skiin' ain't so good!"

It was settled. The general, on McCreary's findings, would leave the Rockies and get his divisions to Alaska to counter the real threat.

As McCreary watched, LaRoy shot to his feet. He backed away from the tank, head cocked to the side. Something had spooked the West Virginian. Or, at least had his attention.

Pearce, getting faint: "*... done well, son. ... We're prayin' for you...*"

"Thank you, sir!" McCreary yelled into the mic. But even his own voice sounded far away. Outside, LaRoy pulled back another step. He dropped one of the rifles and touched the tank's tread with his fingertips. He pulled his hand away, like he'd burned it. Then he reached forward again, and pressed down.

"*...sounds like it's time for wagon's ho!*" Pearce said, a million miles away. "*...we'll give 'em hell! ... good men... very proud...*"

"Thank you, sir," McCreary whispered, as he lowered the mic—just as LaRoy bent his knees and lifted the front end of the tank into the air. Still holding the tank, the young sergeant turned and looked at McCreary through the doorway, puzzled, as though awaiting further instruction. Static rose in McCreary's ear like a spring rain.

"*... saved the republic... grateful... God bless...*"

LaRoy dropped his other rifle and turned his attention back to the tank. Then he flipped the damn thing on its side. Whitefeather lay the Browning on the ground and pulled out his knife. He walked to the upended tank, and as LaRoy watched, the Indian warrior plunged the blade into its bottom panel.

"... *you hear me? ... God bless...*"

With a hiss, and then a spiraling shriek, the tank sagged like a dirty snowball in the sun.

The general.

The army.

North to Alaska—

McCreary whipped back around to the radio equipment. "GENERAL PEARCE!" He didn't know what any of the dials did. "WE WERE WRONG! THERE'S NO ARMY! THERE'S NO BRIDGE! REPEAT—"

The console exploded. He flew backward in a shower of metal and sparks, as Alexander emptied an AK-47 clip into the equipment. McCreary huddled against a desk, arms pressed against the side of his head, as much in shame and defeat than from the noise.

Everything snapped into focus, crashing into McCreary's mind with a sound that was a lot like a Kalashnikov AK-47. What details remained, Alexander would provide him. Alexander liked to talk. And he would remind Lonestar Tactical Unit One, before he killed the bunch of them, that their leader had just cost the United States of America the war.

The barrel of Alexander's AK-47 pressed so far into the underside of McCreary's jaw that the Major could barely breathe. "*Ah, ah, ah!*" he scolded, as he hauled McCreary out of the building, and LaRoy and Whitefeather made an abortive grab for their discarded weapons. McCreary felt no surprise that Alexander spoke in a Russian accent.

"I suggest that you stand back," the spy said, "or I'll silence this American simpleton once and for all. Drop the knife, Tonto." McCreary would have shaken his head in disbelief if the assault rifle had permitted it. They'd been traveling with a Russian spy the whole time.

God, this again?

"Yes, yes," the spy said. "I see that you two enlisted men discovered what your exalted officer and a gentleman could not. The most brilliant ruse in the history of warfare since your own General Patton was given command of the ghost Fifth Army. You Americans have taught us a valuable lesson, but we are the masters." By now, the tank that LaRoy and Whitefeather had killed was a puddle of black and gray rubber. Its two companions, inflated, still looked like the genuine articles.

"You've achieved your mission," Whitefeather said. "Let the man go. We'll turn ourselves in when your friends get here."

Alexander laughed in McCreary's ear. "Ha! Other than myself and this dead comrade, there aren't more than twenty Soviet soldiers within three hundred kilometers of this station. We have thrown everything we have at America. General Pearce took the bait perfectly. Drawing your remaining forces to Alaska will ensure that when the next wave hits, the dottering old fool and his army will be too far away to do any good."

With that, the traitor shoved McCreary forward. He sprawled, ashamed, at Whitefeather's feet. The Indian hauled him up and dusted him off. McCreary spun around. "What's your name?" he asked through gritted teeth.

The spy shifted back into his smooth, American voice: "Why, I'm Robert Alexander, of the Central Intelligence Agency."

"No, you Ruskie son of a bitch… your *real* name."

"Does it matter, Major?" he said, Russian once more. "Feel free to call me… *Aleksandr*." He chuckled and cleared the AK's breech with a loud snap. "You Americans. So focused on *the individual.* What will win this war for us is collective action. The brave Red Army! The ruthless KGB! The noble soldiers I was forced to kill. And most of all, my wife—the beautiful actress of socialist stage and screen… *Valentina Vulvanova.* Each of us is prepared to give everything for the worker's revolution—and Mother Russia!"

"You killed your own wife!" McCreary cried.

"She left the script," Aleksandr said. "To, how you say, improvise. Your night together must have been more than her theater training prepared her for. Do not worry, Major McCreary. I do not take it personally. Her death was one of necessity, not spite."

A female general—of course… *just an actress*. And she'd been killed by her own husband for almost screwing up the role of a lifetime. McCreary chuckled bitterly. "You sure had me goin'," he said. "The best part was arguin' with the command staff against that phony bridge. Gave us something to push against."

"A bridge across the Bering Strait!" the Russian scoffed. "Who would ever think of such a stupid thing? But I knew one man who would find it plausible."

"General Pearce."

"The rugged individual believing in big dreams. The worst American trait of all! But even in putting together our elaborate scheme, we doubted that you would be so stupid as to buy in!"

"But you never shut up about it!" LaRoy said. "The Major's a Texan, and you bein' a smartass just pissed him

104

off. Made him want to crawl to this side of the Strait … just to prove you wrong."

To that, Alexander—*Aleksandr*—smiled with boyish charm, nodded his head, and raised the AK-47. The smug smile was the worst part of all.

"So let me get this straight," Whitefeather said, "all your play acting. A lifetime of sneakin' into the country and workin' your way up the CIA. A phony prison camp with three hundred thousand men flown to Nome twenty or thirty at a time. A couple thousand inflatable tanks. Engineerin' it so we'd come to this very station, the one working transmitter in this part of the world. All of it … to fool our leaders into taking the army north instead of west?"

Aleksandr shrugged and nodded. "Eh, this is true."

"Wouldn't it have been easier just to build the bridge?"

"Silence!" Aleksander commanded. "I am through with your questions!"

"Just one more then," McCreary asked, "that second invasion. Where's it comin' from?"

Aleksandr steadied the AK-47. "You will never know."

Unless he came up with something fast, the game was over. But how bad could that be? Brief pain followed by eternal rest. And when he met Sunny someday on God's golden shore, maybe she'd forgive all he'd done wrong. "Wait," McCreary said. "I need to remove something. The Medal of Honor is sacred. Even a Russian must recognize that."

To McCreary's surprise, Aleksandr nodded with sudden solemnity. "You are correct. Even *I* respect that highest of all decorations. Only the Hero's medal is more exalted. I shall keep your medallion safe—if only for a trophy." He gestured with the barrel. "You may remove it."

McCreary glanced at Whitefeather and LaRoy, each of whom took an almost imperceptible step back. He dug into his collar and slid out the medal. He lifted it over his head and laid it flat in his palm. It glinted dully. Tied to its now now filthy ribbon, knotted with thirteen stars, the five-pointed star glinted.

McCreary looked up from the medal, square in Aleksandr's eyes. "This is going to sting a little," he said, as he twisted his hands and broke the Navy star free from its mount. Aleksandr's eyes narrowed, questioning, as McCreary reared back and spun the Medal of Honor into the Russian spy's neck.

McCreary's aim was true. The points dug into Aleksandr's carotid artery. The spy lowered the AK-47 and, gagging like a stuck pig, clutched at his throat. Blood spurted between his fingers. His bulging eyes made contact with McCreary's.

"At least... I die... in my homeland... McCreary. You... your men... will die far from home..." But Aleksandr's dying speech didn't stop all three Americans from diving for their weapons. Aleksandr sank to his knees just as a hail of AK-47 and Browning .50 caliber rounds echoed into the morning. His body jerked, twitched, and spasmed as the gunfire tore at his clothes and flesh. A minute's hail of lead reduced him into a shimmering pile of ropy goo the color of the Communist banner. McCreary and LaRoy didn't stop firing until their AKs had gone dry; Whitefeather didn't stop until the ground was wet.

Finally, they ended their fury, and the cold Siberian morning was quiet once more. Somewhere in the trees, a bird cawed.

"Well," LaRoy said, ejecting his clip, "that finally shut him up."

* * *

Things were bad.

Marooned in the Soviet Far East. Used as a ploy in a master spy's plan. Winter on its way. And, a half hour after hotfooting it away from the transmitter station, the "Superbridge's" road came to an end. McCreary, LaRoy, and Whitefeather found themselves standing before a wall of trees. They heard breaking waves, somewhere, off to the right. But the ocean had to be at least a couple of miles away, overland.

"What do you think woulda happened if we'd just listened to Alexander?" LaRoy said. The West Virginian walked forward and sat on a high mound of gravel that marked the end of the road. "I know that KGB sonofabitch was goading us to come up here, but what if General Pearce had said, 'Yeah, you're right. Dang Russians can't build anything like that, anyhow!'" LaRoy's eyes lost their focus, and he stared at the ground, smiling at the thought.

"He'd have found another way," McCreary said. "He was smart. I was stupid. Maybe that's the good Lord's way of tellin' us that we had a good run. America, I mean. Mom, apple pie, the flag—all of it."

"No!" Whitefeather's deep baritone echoed through the trees. "Listen to yourself, Major! Our country put men on the moon. We beat the Germans *and* the Japanese. We invented cotton candy, the airplane, and the electric gee-tar. I know we're down, Major, but dadgummit, we've been down before. Now dust yourself off and get us home. Let's win this damn war!"

"This ain't like last time, Charlie," McCreary said. "Your spirit brothers ain't gonna join us in battle. There ain't a bunch of angry hippies in a prison ready to return to God and country. Unless you can find us another army, I'm'a sit this one out."

At that, Whitefeather smiled gently. He lay the squad weapon on the road, closed his eyes, and lifted his chin. He opened his palms and breathed deep; as if in response, a soft wind sifted through the trees. With it came the smell of pine, snow, and the earth itself. The wind teased the soft brim of LaRoy's bushwhacker.

"What's that you doin', Whitefeather?" LaRoy exclaimed. "I thought we was too far from home for all that Injun hocus-pocus!"

The giant sergeant remained in his trance. McCreary peered through the trees. He felt a thousand pair of eyes watching him. He'd read that tigers lived in this part of the world, once, and to this day there were giant bears. Long ago, they ate camels and giant woolly elephants. It occurred to him that Whitefeather's ancestors had walked these grounds, following those elephants to a real superbridge, one made of land. As the wind hissed through the trees, McCreary swore he heard something buried deep within it—whispers, ancient songs, the bouncing heartbeat of a drum.

As quick as it had arisen, the wind died down. Whitefeather's deep brown eyes opened slowly.

McCreary heard a growl. He spun around and looked into the golden glare of a huge gray wolf. The animal stood ten feet away. It looked like a statue, all four legs atop a flat stump. The animal stared, breathing in long and slow. McCreary froze. He'd never seen a wolf before. He'd always assumed they'd be a little burlier than a coyote, but this thing was larger than a Great Dane.

Off to McCreary's right, LaRoy backed away, his feet crunching the gravel. "Nice doggie," he said quietly. The wolf turned its head to him with alarming speed, ears up. It opened its maw and showed a row of sharp teeth.

"*Freeze*," McCreary hissed.

"It's all right, sir," Whitefeather said. "There are friends nearby. At the shore. Our visitor here will lead us to 'em." McCreary turned from the wolf and looked at Whitefeather, whose eyes had regained their focus. Whitefeather picked up his weapon like it was a toy and, instead of aiming at the wolf, slung it over his shoulder.

McCreary's head went back and forth between Whitefeather and the wolf, which was now panting like a blue-tick hound. "Friends? What kinds of friends?"

Whitefeather shrugged. Whether he knew the answer or was just joshing, McCreary didn't know.

"How's this mutt supposed to find us some friends?" LaRoy asked.

"I'm sorry, fellas." Whitefeather smiled. "That's all I can tell you right now."

McCreary backed away from the wolf. "Whitefeather, this is crazy—"

But he was cut short by a streak of fur and muscle, as the wolf leapt across the road into the brush. There came a whoop, the one LaRoy had learned from the Comanches back at the Battle of Wrangler Plains.

"You heard the man, Major!" he said. "Let's follow this pooch! There's still friends we ain't met yet! Come on! We're wastin' daylight!"

Before he was done speaking, LaRoy had vanished into the trees. McCreary and Whitefeather heard him laughing, whooping, and making enough noise to attract a hundred Soviet divisions. If only they'd existed.

DAY SEVEN

Sept. 27, 1989
Bering seacoast
Magadan Oblast

"A Soviet submarine?"

McCreary put his binoculars down and hunkered back behind the rocks. Whitefeather's spiritual antennae were either broken or worth about the same as a dowsing rod. Far below them, anchored close to the steep shoreline, lay a black submarine, longer than a football field. Sinuous waves traversed its length, hypnotically.

Whitefeather peered down at the water, his face scratched and bug-bit like the others. It had been a long slog down the rocky coastal slope, and a frigid night spent in survival shelters made of pine boughs. At times over the course of the trek, the wolf had periodically disappeared into the woods, and then reappeared whenever they wandered off the trail. Now the wolf was gone. In its absence the smell of the North Pacific had drawn them forward.

On its bow, the men could read the sub's blocky, Russian name: Потёмкин.

What did it mean? *Pottery? Postman? Potomac?* McCreary's rudimentary grasp of Cyrillic had blown away in the ocean breeze. Why didn't the Russians write like normal people?

"Those are our new friends, huh?" he muttered, glaring at Whitefeather. "Any chance of getting that flea-bit mutt back here so I can ask him what the hell we're supposed to do now?"

"The wolf did his part." Whitefeather shrugged. "Who knows, Major, maybe they're friendly Russians."

"They're all strapped. Every single one." McCreary studied the launch that hummed from the sub to the pebbled beach. Inside the boat sat six armed sailors in their blue uniforms with the horizontal stripes along the neck. They would join a complement of two-dozen comrades huddled around a campfire. The advance party had slaughtered and dressed a couple of deer. The waft of sizzling venison made McCreary's mouth water.

McCreary handed LaRoy the binoculars. LaRoy whistled softly. "Is that sub a fake, too? Those damn Russians can make an inflatable anything!"

Whitefeather chuckled. "They'd probably make you one of them blow-up girlfriends, if you ask 'em friendly enough."

"If it's fake, it should win a prize ," McCreary said. He took the binoculars back and studied some more. "No, that's a real boat, all right. *Akula* class."

"I thought we sunk all their submarines," LaRoy said.

"We sank most of their boomers, their big missile subs, but this'n is built to sink ships," McCreary said. "Got himself in a fight, though. He's missin' a chunk outta his starboard bow. Conning tower's shot to hell. There's a line of 110mm hits. I'm amazed the damn thing's still afloat."

With the smell of venison, now came the sounds of an accordion and drunken singing. The Reds were having a fine little party down on the beach. The only things missing were the girls in bikinis.

McCreary stood wearily. "All right, you two: time's wastin'. We're gonna get on that sub."

"Lets see," LaRoy said, getting to his feet. "So far, you've stole an airplane, a Russian spy's wife, and now you want a submarine."

"I'm not going to steal no sub," McCreary said, slinging his AK-47. "Just some airtime on the radio."

They staggered back up the hill—and walked right into a squad of Soviet marines.

There were eight of them, each in the same blue-striped shirts and gray coats of their comrades on the beach. They were gaunt, hollow-cheeked. All of them were so pale they glowed in the afternoon sun; they must have been submerged for months. The youngest man, barely out of his teens, was the only one unarmed. Over his shoulder, he'd slung two dirty burlap sacks, bulging with tubers and roots. The closest sailor, the oldest, glared at McCreary and spat. The armed sailors cocked their AK-47s.

"Whitefeather, LaRoy—drop 'em," McCreary said. Each Lonestar member put his weapon on the hard ground and put his hands on his head.

"Bandity!" the closest man hissed.

LaRoy whispered, "They think we're bandits."

"Thanks for the translation," Whitefeather muttered.

The sailors froze. One by one, they looked at each other, at Lonestar, then back at each other.

"You ... John Wayne?" the lead man asked.

113

"McCreary, Michael J., United States Army—"

"*Amerikanskiy!*" each cried, almost in unison.

"We sure have a knack for getting captured, Major," LaRoy said, ruefully. But the Russians dropped their weapons and rushed forward. They encircled Whitefeather's massive chest in a group hug. They then joined hands and danced around him, circling to some chanted song, feet kicking every which way.

"They're not capturing us," McCreary said. Two more men threw their arms around him and jumped up and down. "They're surrendering."

The Russians built a bonfire the size of the Great Pyramid and cooked a feast. In addition to taking a couple of deer, the sailors had bagged a half-ton moose. The Russians were inventive with the roots dug up on their latest forage, and each member of Lonestar dined on a mess of stew that McCreary's mother would've seen fit to serve Pastor Joe at Sunday dinner.

Sixty or seventy yards off shore, the submarine guarded the entrance to the cove. The water got deep out there, it looked like. That, or the Russians had run aground. Hiding. From someone.

It was only on his third helping of stew, sitting on a bleached log next to the water, that McCreary realized he'd been eating off officers' china. And there wasn't an officer in sight.

McCreary leaned over to Whitefeather. "What'd the lead Ivan say his name was?"

"Yevgeny," Whitefeather said, not pausing as he shoveled stew.

"Hey, Yevgeny," McCreary said, balancing his bowl on a rock. "Where's the officers?"

Yevgeny had been ladling stew out of a giant pot. He misunderstood McCreary and advanced with another ladleful. "More, *Amerikanskiy*!" All smiles, yellow teeth.

McCreary patted his belly and stood. "*Nyet, nyet… Ya polon*! I'm looking for officers! Uh… *Kapitan*!" He looked around in exaggerated fashion, where the two-dozen sailors reclined around the bonfire. They smoked bitter cigarettes, played cards, or lay passed out, sailor's caps over their eyes, bottles of vodka against their chest.

Yevgeny's smile grew sad. "*Nyet, Amerikanskiy*," he said. "*Nyet kapitan*."

"Just wonderin' where he is, is all."

The sailor nodded up and behind McCreary's right shoulder. He and the rest of his outfit had somehow missed a horrific sight coming down the path. Far up the cliff stood a giant, dead tree the shape of a crucifix. Four men hung from it, hands tied behind their backs, cloth bags over their heads. Three of the men wore the blue uniforms and gray overcoats of the Soviet Navy; the fourth wore bloody cook's whites.

McCreary looked around for his AK-47. It rested next to the now reclining LaRoy and Whitefeather.

"Do not worry, *Amerikanskiy*," the sailor said. "*You* did not abuse us. *You* did not force us to take double watch next to leaking reactor!"

"Nor did *you* feed us meat, infested with worms!" said another man. A group of ten men closed in.

"The *kapitan*, he surfaced and declared that twenty of us would be shot! Threw us under tarp!"

"We took over ship!" said another man. "We *all* officers now!" The men cheered. A few threw their hats. It was on this beach, McCreary decided, that the worker's revolution had died—and been reborn.

"Mutiny," McCreary declared above their boisterous laughter.

"Mutiny!" Yevgeny said. "*Da*—mutiny!"

"Who's in charge?" McCreary asked. "Is it you? Or you?"

Yevgeny sighed and folded his hands together. He rested his arms on his knees and addressed McCreary like a father to a child: "*Amerikanskiy*, there is no new *kapitan*. We have Lieutenant Romanenko. He sees what we do to other officers and *zambolit* and wisely he joins us. But if he takes *kapitan* rank, he, too, will hang from cross!"

McCreary couldn't get his bearings. The war in America made some sort of crazy sense, but out here, things were unraveling. There was only one part that he understood anymore: the need to tell General Pearce about the phony invasion in Alaska. "I need a radio. And I need you to take me to your lieutenant."

And it was here, of course, that McCreary finally noticed a few AK-47s in the crowd of sailors that slowly closed in. Two of them rudely roused Whitefeather and LaRoy, who had set their plates in the sand and had been trying to doze off. The Russians, now angry, ordered Whitefeather and LaRoy to stand. "You Americans," Yevgeny sighed. "Always asking questions. Always asking for favors. Always asking for *thinks*. We already have given you our food and our music."

A short, stocky Russian with a heavy, bristly black beard tugged on Yevgeny's arm and spoke quick and quiet into his ear. A smile broke across Yevgeny's cracked, yellow teeth. Both men laughed.

"*Sasha!*" Yevgeny cried. A wave of laughter now spread through the sailors. McCreary felt a rifle butt in his lower back. He was shoved to where Whitefeather and LaRoy stood.

"Sasha!" cried the man with the beard.

"SASHA!" cried the sailors in unison. McCreary felt his arms yanked behind him, then the cold steel of handcuffs. They did the same to Whitefeather and LaRoy, and now shoved the American trio toward the launches. McCreary craned his neck furiously, looking for Yevgeny. "Sasha? Who's Sasha?" McCreary asked.

"No, no," Yevgeny said somewhere behind him as they reached the boats. "Proper name is *Big* Sasha. And you: Big Sasha will enjoy a whole lot!" More laughter.

"Welp," LaRoy sighed wearily, as the sailors shoved them into the center launch, "looks like we're captured again!"

The ride out to the giant sub took less than a minute. Until they were right up on it, the craft's size was difficult to comprehend. An *Akula*-class boat stretched over three hundred feet. The conning tower was the size of a small office building. As the launches rounded the starboard bow, McCreary felt intimidation at the sheer size of it all. Maybe that was the idea.

The sub was parked in a large, circular cove, maybe a half-mile wide, with a narrow opening to the Pacific in the distance. They were hidden from all but the most committed aircraft. Also, the calm water made life aboard a surfaced submarine somewhat bearable. Indeed, this was the perfect place to stage a mutiny.

Getting onto the sub with his hands bound was difficult. McCreary was alternately shoved from behind and pulled from above. The short deck in front of the conning tower was narrow, perhaps forty feet long and fifteen feet wide before it sloped precipitously into the water. Once his feet were under him and he stood on the metal deck, McCreary turned, expecting to see

117

Whitefeather and LaRoy next to him. Instead, he saw that they were still on the launch. Five crew joined him on the deck, while the rest of the boats formed a perimeter around the bow.

Clutching the Texan's arm, Yevgeny called to the top of the conning tower.

"Sasha!"

One of the other sailors unlocked McCreary's cuffs. McCreary instinctively surveyed the deck, and the prospects of escape. He might have a chance against a few of these men; they were pale and malnourished from months under the waves. But two of them were armed, and if he managed to overpower them, what then? Besides, Whitefeather and LaRoy were still cuffed in the boats. McCreary pictured them drowning in the cold water, arms behind their backs thousands of miles from home. For their sake, he accepted the inevitable. Whatever the inevitable was.

"Sasha!" Yevgeny cried again.

A second later, McCreary saw a large, shadowy head and shoulders appear, silhouetted from behind by the sun.

"Da!" came a deep, rumbling baritone.

For at least thirty seconds, Yevgny and the mysterious Sasha conversed in Russian. There was something strange about Sasha's voice, a quality McCreary couldn't place. McCreary looked to Whitefeather and LaRoy. Both men looked at each other with what looked like a mix of amusement and alarm—were they following the conversation? Did they understand some passel of Russian that McCreary didn't know about? Then it occurred to him that the light was different where they were. They could see what McCreary could not. Laughter spread amongst the sailors again, both those in the launches and the handful on deck. Finally, the shadowy figure on the conning tower accepted Yevgeny's offer with a sigh. He wiped his hands on a cloth, then swung a huge, thick leg over the edge and began the climb down.

"You will fight Big Sasha, *Amerikanskiy!* For our amusement, yes? If you win, we take you to see Lieutenant Romanenko. If you lose, Big Sasha will throw you into water—and your men will go in after you. Until you drown."

"This is barbaric," McCreary said. "I demand to see your commanding officer. That's an order, Chief!"

Yevgeny leaned in. "You are not in a position to give orders, *Amerikanskiy*. Your rank entitles you only to swing from tree with others!"

Above them, legs and heavy boots thumped down the ladder. Big Sasha landed heavily on the deck. McCreary saw the source of the amusement.

Big Sasha was a woman.

She stood at least six-six, with thick, greasy cropped black hair. Huge and menacing but unmistakably female. She wore greasy coveralls and smelled of diesel. And when she looked at McCreary, the big girl smiled wide, showing two rows of small, yellow teeth.

"Behold Sasha!" Yevgeny said to the world. "Proud daughter of Volgograd! Winner two gold medals at Moscow Olympics! Finest product of Socialist sports machine!"

Socialist sports machine. So that was it. Take your typical burly Russian gal and pump her full of a cocktail of testosterone, bull-piss, and pride in the Motherland.

"Holy smokes, would you look at her!" LaRoy shouted. "Now *that's* the kind of Russian woman I been hearin' about!"

"Sasha!" Yevgeny ordered. *"Prikhodi igrats nashimi amerikanskimi drugu!"*

Out on the boats, the sailors' laughter boiled over. McCreary was shoved forward by the butt of an AK as Yevgeny and his men climbed carefully down the bow into their launch. McCreary looked at his men and held his hands up. Whitefeaher smirked. "Keep your hands up, Major," he said. "Don't worry about us. Just hit her harder than she hits you!"

Hit a woman? *Never!* McCreary stepped toward Whitefeather's boat, ignoring Sasha completely. "No way! I ain't hittin' no g—"

Sasha's fist crashed into McCreary's face right below his right eye. The sailors erupted in cheers. McCreary spun and landed on his back. For a moment, he passed out from the impact and pain. As consciousness flickered back, McCreary reached to his face and felt the slick flow of blood. Above him, Sasha loomed, giant fists balled. Her smile hadn't broke one bit.

"Get up, Yankee!" Yevgeny cried somewhere. "Sasha, she like you! She want to play, eh? *Heh heh heh!*"

McCreary rolled to his side and tried to stand. He wasn't surprised when Sasha's boot slammed into his gut. Breath knocked entirely away, McCreary spun like a log. The deck's flat surface gave way to a hard slope all the way down to the water. McCreary reached out blindly with his left hand and caught an exposed loop of pipe, stopping his fall. He began pulling himself back to the deck when Sasha's boot pressed onto his knuckles. McCreary screamed. Bone ground into bone, tendons stretched.

Determination boiled up out of nowhere like a Texas gusher. McCreary pulled himself up to his knees and punched the back of Sasha's knee. With a yelp of pain that was low and strong and somehow still feminine, she collapsed on her back, wide mouth open to the sky. McCreary freed his left hand and crawled back to the deck. He stood over Sasha, fists balled up at his sides. He knew that at least one Russian word was the same as English:

"Stop!" he ordered. *"Nyet bor'ba!"* No fight!

Sasha met his glare. Her considerable brow furrowed. With alarming speed, her boot swept behind McCreary and took out his knees. He fell on his backside to another chorus of Russian laughter. Within a half second, McCreary was back on his feet, wincing at the pain of his twisted left hand. McCreary raised his fists around his head.

Mindful of the dropoff to the water, McCreary kept up his hands and circled to the right. Sasha circled, as well, her back to the water. McCreary missed a flicker of opportunity—*I should have charged right there and knocked this fair maiden into the drink.* But the chance came and went. Now, their positions were reversed, McCreary's back to the conning tower and Sasha's to the sloping bow.

The time for games was over. McCreary advanced. Sasha responded with an expert, tactical withdrawal. McCreary readied for a strike—then stopped again.

He couldn't do it. Couldn't strike a woman. He thought of Sunny. Sure she was prettier than this'n. But they were all part of the same side of the coin. Meant to be protected by men, not hurt by them.

Ah, the human female, McCreary mused grimly, his attack in a holding pattern, *source of a man's strength—and his weakness!*

Then, another side of his mind, the *proper* side, answered with a masculine call. *Stop your dilly-dallying.*

Show this unholy Communist she-creature the righteous power of the American male!

"All right, Missy," McCreary said, *"I tried to be a gentleman."*

McCreary jabbed. He caught her upper jaw. Sasha's eyes flew open. She staggered back and put her mouth to her hand. Blood.

She'll give up. She ain't got the stomach for a real fight.

Sasha clenched her bloody teeth and lunged. She tackled McCreary like a Dallas Cowboy linebacker. Down he went. His already aching vertebrae crunched between the sub's outer hull and Sasha's two-hundred-some-odd pounds. In less than a second, she had him on his stomach. Her sturdy, tree-trunk thighs wrapped around his neck from behind. To the sounds of cheering Russians and the stiffening Arctic breeze, Big Sasha girded her loins and squeezed.

McCreary's head swelled like a red weather balloon. He reached up and tried to pry Sasha's thighs off his neck. Any moment, he expected a hail of fists and eye-gouging. But Sasha was content to squeeze.

Somewhere over the sound of blood rushing into his head, McCreary could hear the old girl laugh. It was a rich baritone, filled with faux-masculine strength and Socialist triumph. McCreary wasn't sure which infuriated him more.

He let go of her thighs, reached back blindly, and struck with his fists in unison. Miraculously, under those coveralls, the ravages of sports science, and God knew what else, Sasha still retained some traces of womanhood. He felt his fists strike something akin to breasts. Sasha bellowed in pain, but her thighs remained affixed. He hit her again, and again, and again.

Finally, her thighs loosened enough for McCreary to wriggle free. He rolled away and almost tumbled off the hull. He wobbled to his feet as Sasha struggled to hers. The old girl's hair was tousled and slicked with sweat. Blood smeared her lower jaw. Her face was red, and veins throbbed blue along her temples. McCreary had his back to the ocean; if she charged him, he could sidestep. Instead, she did something far more dangerous. She advanced, slowly. McCreary raised his fists, but they were useless as the big Russian gal reached out and took him in a bear hug.

McCreary struggled to escape. He felt his boots lift off the deck. His feet dangled. Sasha's strategy was clear: make him pass out, then toss his useless pink body into the drink. With dots clouding his vision, McCreary studied Sasha's huge brown eyes.

What did they do to you, old girl? he found himself wondering as consciousness left him. *After they pumped you full of man juice and made you compete under the Communist star, what good were you going to be? How much feminine fulfillment were you supposed to find in the bowels of a submarine?*

Here was a woman who would never know a man's strong caress. Would never take his seed. Bear his children.

Maybe if…

No. Anything but that!

But it was the only way. It was time to take one for the team.

McCreary braced what little strength he had in his right foot, pressed forward, and titled his head. He planted a passionate kiss on Sasha's mouth.

Her python-like arms loosened. The pressure on McCreary's body eased. But he wasn't finished. McCreary

123

forced his tongue between the big Russian's lips. He was simultaneously pleased and sickened that she took him willingly. For an eternal moment, their tongues pressed and slid together. Finally, his bile rising, McCreary pulled away from Sasha's collapsing grasp. Her eyes lost focus. She staggered. Her heavy eyelids fluttered. When she regained her balance, she locked eyes on McCreary and smiled dreamily.

Out in the boats, no one made a sound.

McCreary launched himself into her midsection. She exclaimed in surprise—her baritone rising to a sad tenor. Sasha stumbled, rumbled, then tumbled backward. She took one hard spill, clanged off the hull, and hit the choppy waves with a mighty splash.

Out in the boats, the sailors cried out in protest. They cursed McCreary in Russian, spitting in his direction, and made violent, dismissive gestures. On the deck, McCreary wiped his mouth and tongue with the back of his filthy sleeve. Then he pointed at the launch where LaRoy and Whitefeather waited, arms still bound. "Release them!" he commanded.

Yevgeny was furious. He stood in the launch. "Not fair, *Amerikanskiy*. That is not how you win fight!"

"I'm a lover, not a fighter," McCreary said. He pointed at his men again. "Do it!"

Meanwhile, Big Sasha had paddled over to the nose and crawled her way onto its tapered surface. Shivering, broken-hearted, she pushed herself to a sitting position, huge head between her knees. Her shoulders trembled. Defeat ran off her broad back like a waterfall. For a brief moment, McCreary had given her a glimpse at what another woman might feel every day. Sasha cried.

She was a lady, after all.

* * *

As he descended the ladder into darkness, it occurred to McCreary that he might be the first American military man to see the inside of a Soviet submarine. The novelty wore off immediately. The air was fetid, a mix of diesel oil, metal shavings, and flatulence. Yevgeny, waiting for him in the access tunnel, beckoned from the shadows, still plainly disgusted. "This way, *Amerikanskiy.*"

"What about my men? You gave me your word."

"They will be along soon," Yevgeny said. "When a Russian gives you his word, he gives you his soul."

"That's what you fellas said at the peace talks in '85," McCreary muttered. "That didn't work out so well for us."

"That was politicians," Yevgeny said as he stepped through a bulkhead door. "You and me, we are pawns, *eh?*"

McCreary had to duck so much under the bulkheads and pipes that he adopted a crouching lope as he followed the Russian sailor. The lighting did not improve as he navigated through rooms and tunnels, and down ladders. It became a blur of shadows and pipes, valves and dials. He and Yevgeny descended one more ladder into a green-hued command room. The ship's officers hadn't gone quietly. Holes from automatic weapons peppered every surface. Every computer terminal was shattered. Glass littered the metal decking, sprinkling the sticky pools of blood.

"You boys had yourselves quite a fight," McCreary said.

Yevgeny didn't answer. He led McCreary across the room to a metal door. Someone inside listened to a warbly phonograph. The music was at once booming and restrained, powerful and sad, the kind of thing Russians played at Communist rallies. It brought to mind parades of soldiers and missiles and tanks through Red Square. McCreary stepped through the door.

It had been the captain's quarters. A Soviet lieutenant with a trim beard sat behind a compact but ornate wooden desk, drinking vodka. A Makarov pistol lay next to the bottle. The lieutenant looked up as the two men entered. He saw McCreary and bolted to his feet.

Yevgeny stood at attention and spoke to the lieutenant in Russian. He mimed their encounter on the cliffs above the beach. Then, at the mention of the name *Sasha,* he swung his fists, re-enacting a frantic, fumbling boxing match. His expression melted into disgust—he finished by miming a hug and a kiss. With a sneer, he then presented McCreary, and stepped back.

The Soviet officer's expression hardened through most of the speech, then gave way to resignation. "I am Lieutenant Pavel Romanenko, last remaining officer of the Soviet submarine K-617 *Potemkin,*" the man finally said.

"Major Michael McCreary, United States Army."

Romanenko smirked at McCreary's filthy, non-descript fatigues and lack of emblem. "Given our respective ranks and my current situation," the Russian officer said, "I am not sure who should salute the other."

McCreary stuck out his hand. "I'm not sure it matters much anymore, Lieutenant. Looks like the war may be over for the both of us."

Romanenko looked at him askance, but shook his hand. "Chief Surayev informs me that you have … encountered one of my crew on our bow. Had I known of such a contest, I would have put a stop to its indignities. Please, have a seat. It would appear that we have much to discuss."

McCreary hesitated. "How is it you're not hangin' from a tree with the rest?"

"Lieutenant Romanenko was kinder to us than others, so we spared noose," Yevgeny answered. "But be warned, *Mayór* McCreary. As we Russians say, Death answers before it is asked."

Romanenko's first move was to discretely put the Markov back in the desk, and to offer McCreary a shot of vodka. The Texan politely refused. When the Soviet officer asked him rapid questions about his presence in Siberia, McCreary— now seated with Yevgeny standing behind him—grinned faintly and recited name, rank, and serial number.

Romanenko waved it all away with his hand. "Let us get to the point: it is plain to see that you have learned about our... *inflated* capabilities in the Soviet Far East."

McCreary nodded. "And it looks like your fancy plans to ... *build a bridge between our two countries*... are a mite farfetched. For this century, anyway."

Romanenko paused, then replied, "Perhaps someday."

"Why did your men mutiny?"

Romanenko downed a shot of vodka, and poured another. "There were... abuses," Romanenko said.

When the Soviets attacked the United States, Romanenko explained, *Potemkin* had been part of a reserve fleet, with orders to sink any and all American shipping. Romanenko recited the *Potemkin's* kills: the *U.S.S. Nimitz,* three destroyers, and two Princess cruise ships. But the fleet's rickety submarines began to break down. Fatigued, battling leaky reactors and eating from rotting stores, the crews rebelled.

During a refueling stop in Archangelsk, the captain refused to grant his men shore leave. The sailors spoke openly of mutiny. They presented a list of demands to the officers. The captain had heard that the city's population, thousands of miles from Moscow and cut off from Soviet interference, was experimenting with free enterprise and religious freedom. In response, the captain personally shot the leader of the mutinous sailors and dumped his body in town as a warning not only to the crew but to the entire city. The civilians mourned, but when the funeral became too religious for Archangelsk's political officer, he and the *Potemkin's* captain ordered the Soviet police to open fire. One woman carrying an armload of religious tracts and a homemade business license permit to the city hall was shot through her spectacles. The policeman who shot her also bayoneted her baby stroller as it bounced down the steps. This as a lesson to capitalism and God Himself.

The sailors rebelled again. This time they overpowered the crew after a bloody gun battle on the bridge that left much of the ship's electronics destroyed. Romanenko always had curried favor with the crew, and because of this was the only officer left alive.

The *Potemkin* steamed out of port. It found itself in the middle of the last three cruisers in the entire Soviet navy. One of the ships refused to fire on their own sub. The other ships sent it to the bottom. In the fight that followed, the mutinous *Potemkin* sank the remaining boats. But it sustained damage of its own. Now, it was barely seaworthy. The crew had intended the cove as a final resting place—after the crew executed the captive cook and the sub's officers.

"It would appear that we are in a similar situation," Romanenko said finally. "You are far from home. We cannot return, either."

"What if I offered you asylum," McCreary said. "The war is over for both of us. Let's head back to the States. You'll be safe there."

Romanenko interrupted him: "Out of the question. We trust neither you nor this vessel."

Yevgeny argued with Romanenko in Russian. The lieutenant responded in English: "And you are free to kill me, Chief Surayev, but I am the only surviving navigator!" He returned his attention to McCreary, and smiled. "Unless you Americans also have served in the navy, your men would not survive the trip without my assent."

McCreary had to think. With the radio destroyed, there was no way to reach General Pearce. The U.S. army was no doubt at the Canadian border by now, chasing an army that wasn't there. This would leave the rest of America open to God knew what.

Unless…

McCreary's thoughts turned to home. To towering mountains, fields that might someday again yield grain, to an America that might one day return to greatness under the Stars and Stripes.

And to beaches. Miles and miles of warm, sandy beaches.

McCreary reached into his pocket. He ran his thumb over the Medal of Honor's rounded points, still crusted with Communist blood.

The images swelled within him.

"Lieutenant," McCreary said, "I'd like to propose a deal. I wanna take you boys to a place Russians dream about when they're linin' up to buy day old bread. A place where a man can be his own boss—or work for minimum wage, because he can get a Big Mac for a buck-sixty-nine. Where he can drive a pickup truck to a swimmin' hole with a beer in his lap, a good huntin' dog ridin' shotgun, and his best girl sittin' smack dab in the middle. I wanna take you to a land of towering mountains, crystal rivers, and forests that provide scenic beauty—while also giving us products that all of us can use and enjoy. A place where he can choose to attend the church of his choice. Where he can dig his toes into a deep shag carpet while watchin' football on a color TV the size of meat locker. I wanna take you boys to the Super Bowl, the Indy 500, and the Bassmasters Championships. Fellas, stick with me, and I'll show you a place where the only worker's paradise you'll ever need... is a corner bar after quittin' time."

McCreary knew he had Yevgeny from the way the Russian chief had sat down hard halfway through his speech, shaking his head at the wonders the Texan had described. Romanenko shook his head skeptically.

Only God in heaven knew what choices were running through that Russian head of his.

DAY EIGHT

Sept. 28, 1989
K-617 Potemkin
North Pacific Ocean

The sub plowed through icy seas, under a slate sky that turned the waves to the color of charcoal. McCreary, Romanenko, Yevgeny, and Whitefeather stood on the conning tower as the Soviet lieutenant scanned the horizon through binoculars. Below decks, LaRoy helped the sailors through a mad dash of repairs that might allow the ship to submerge.

Agitated, Romanenko lowered his binoculars and let them hang against the front of his thick wool coat. "We should have stayed in the cove," he said. "We are naked on the surface. Defenseless!"

"How many torpedoes do you have left?" McCreary asked.

Romanenko didn't answer for a moment, then said, "Five. Conventional, not nuclear. One of the few treaty terms we honored."

McCreary scanned the waves with binoculars of his own. The rough sea was empty. For now.

"Just so we are clear," Romanenko said, "when we dock in Los Angeles, we will scuttle the ship so that neither side may use it. My men will be safe, and all of us will escape imprisonment."

"That's the deal," McCreary said. "An American keeps his word. Your crew knows that."

"What they know," Romanenko said, "is that California is the home of beautiful women, sports cars, and blue jeans."

"One thing I never understood," Whitefeather asked. "Why did you Russians leave Los Angeles alone? The rest of the Western states are crawlin' with Communists."

"Such decisions were above my rank," Romanenko said. "Moscow ordered our military to take the American Mainland but leave a perimeter around Southern California. In return for their help in disabling your nuclear forces, the Chinese asked for Hawaii and Australia. This is all we were told. In the Soviet Navy, it is best to follow orders and refrain from asking questions."

The big Indian smiled back, nonplussed: "Good thing I'm not in the Soviet Navy."

LaRoy's West Virginia drawl came over the intercom: "Ready in twenty minutes, Major! Y'all best come downstairs less'n you wanna swim to L.A.!"

"I don't like this, Major," Whitefeather said above the quickening gale. "An ill wind is blowin'. It tells me we're headin' into a heap o' trouble."

"After the week we've had?" McCreary joked. "Nothin' we can't handle."

Romanenko scanned the horizon once more and then moved below decks. Whitefeather joined him. For a few minutes more, McCreary stayed put, a lone figure on an enemy sub in the middle of a cold ocean, straining through his binoculars to glimpse a shore that lay thousands of miles over the horizon.

It was California or bust.

DAY THIRTEEN

Oct. 3, 1989
K-617 Potemkin
North Pacific Ocean

They spotted the Chinese ship about five hundred miles due east of Hawaii.

Two days after leaving the Soviet Far East, work crews aboard the *Potemkin* managed to keep the sub no more than fifty meters below the waves. Whenever Romanenko ordered it deeper, an ominous series of groans and tremors shook the sub. The crew, cut by a third since the mutiny, did their jobs with a lazy efficiency that McCreary found off-putting. There was none of that hustle that one might see in an American aircrew. What was missing was the spark of individual initiative—with their free health care, education, and whatever else it was that Mother Russia provided from cradle to grave, without requiring that they work for it.

Yevgeny had been scanning the surface through the periscope, when he exclaimed in Russian. Romanenko nudged him aside, looked for himself. Startled, he, too, shouted orders.

"*Kitayskiy voyennyy korabl'vpered! V dvukh kilometrakh! Klass Predsedatel Mao!*"

McCreary, watching from the weapons station, had picked up enough Russian over the past two days to know that Romanenko wanted the Soviet sub to stop completely. McCreary moved forward and peered through the scope. He couldn't believe his eyes.

"You are getting a privileged view, Major McCreary," he heard Romanenko say. "That is a Chairman Mao–class battlecruiser. The pride of the Chinese navy. Its engineers and the thousands of workers who built it were put to death to maintain secrecy. And then the executioners were themselves put to death."

McCreary blinked and studied the ship again. It was a massive sculpture of squarish, winglike sails, atop a curved, all-metal hull. The sails had long, horizontal support beams, parallel to each other. The heavy seas topside didn't bother the giant ship at all. The floating nightmare split the waves like a Ginsu knife.

"Why, it's like an old Chinese junk!" McCreary exclaimed.

Somewhere, he swore he could hear the faint, menacing sound of a gong.

"No," Romanenko said, "it is a *Megajunk*. Modern. Wind-powered so that it requires no fuel. Two hundred meters long, with fully battened alloy sails that scrape the clouds. Crew of fifteen hundred sailors and marines. More weaponry than any warship ever put to sea."

A panicked sonar crewman looked up from his scope. "The ship is approaching!" he said in English.

"All-stop!" Romanenko commanded. He turned to McCreary. "The ship's harmonic detection equipment is advanced but flawed. If we do not move, they may not know we are here."

"How many torpedoes did you say you have left?" McCreary asked.

"Five," Romanenko said. "But it is irrelevant. Against a ship with their countermeasures, we would have to fire at point blank range."

McCreary studied the Soviet officer, who was visibly uncomfortable at the thought. "Then we fire it at point blank range! That ship is hostile and we need to sink her!"

Romanenko scowled. But before he could answer, a crewman shouted: "Lieutenant Romanenko! The Chinese ship has turned toward us. Range, fifteen hundred meters!"

"*Der'mo!*" Romanenko exclaimed. "We are not prepared for this!"

At that point, a voice sounded over the *Potemkin's* speakers. The voice was lilting. Thin. Almost musical. *Chinese!* The speaker was male, McCreary believed, but he couldn't tell much else about it. The crewmen looked at each other, confused. How had this message come over their speakers?

After a pause, more speech.

This time in Russian. The crewmembers sat up straight, looked at each other, panicked expressions spreading beneath their heavy brows. They murmured to each other, frantically.

Romanenko shushed them, just as the message came over in accented English:

"*Submarine* Potemkin," the voice said. "*This message is for you: we know of your betrayal and are working on your location. Show yourself! Surrender! Or we shall take great satisfaction in blowing you out of the water.*"

"The Chinese are clever," Romanenko said. "Good with computers, as America found out on the first day of the war, yes? Within a year or two, such a craft might remotely be able to take over the entire workings of our ship. As of now, they only can blindly broadcast over our communication systems."

McCreary peered through the periscope again, and saw the junk bearing down on them, its massive sail slats turning this way and that to catch the wind. An array of Type 79 and Type 81 twin 100mm guns swung forward. The decks bristled with Silkworm anti-ship missiles. As for their anti-submarine capabilities, McCreary didn't want to guess. He caught sight of white-uniformed men on deck. Dozens of them. No, hundreds! One in particular—a tall man, decked out in red silk robes, with a long, flowing, string mustache. The figure stood on the ship's jutting bow, hands on his hips, wind coursing through his long hair. Hanging from a bright red sash was a long, curved sword.

"*Where are you, submarine* Potemkin?" came the voice again. "*Betrayers of the Revolution! If you are nearby, Lieutenant Romanenko, our Soviet friends have told us all about you! We smell your bourgeois stench, and wait for the opportunity to send you to a cold, watery death!*"

Romanenko's expression fell. He was now a traitor. And somehow, everyone in the Communist Party knew it.

"Best lower this peeper, Lieutenant," McCreary said to Romanenko. "It's kill or be killed. They're on their way."

Romanenko took a peek, swore again, then hit the switch lowering the periscope. He gave the order to power down all systems. "That man on the bow," Romanenko said. "He is their commander. Each ship has one, similarly powerful. Skilled in all of the Asian martial arts, and in the use of a sword. A hint of what we are up against, Major. Perhaps surrender…"

McCreary glanced at the crew, all of whom studied the two of them. "You surrender this boat to the Chinese," McCreary muttered, "there won't be anything left of you to feed the fish. Your men will see to that."

Before Romanenko could answer, a steady, throbbing hum coursed through the ship. The junk's engines rose in pitch, until the sub was filled with a sound like the roar of a 747. The sailors looked around in panic. One man prayed and made the Orthodox sign of the cross. Romanenko silenced him with a swat across the back of the head.

Ten minutes stretched into an hour. The sub's interior was silent, lit only by a few red LEDs on the control screens. McCreary waited for the inevitable depth charges.

The minutes ticked by, until the thrum of the junk's engines faded. Minutes later, silence. Perhaps the Chinese ship wasn't so confident in their proximity after all.

Finally, Romanenko dared to raise the periscope, and at last confirmed that the monster craft's sails were disappearing over the horizon.

"Rulevoy Ivanov," Romanenko commanded at a bespectacled helmsman. *"Ustanovit' kurs na tridtsati trekh gradusov shiroty, otritsatel'noy sto dvadtsat' gradusov dolgoty!"*

He turned back to McCreary, "There are the final coordinates for Los Angeles," he said, as the sub swung slowly to the southeast. "Now, let us pray to your Capitalist gods that Hawaii was enough to satisfy the Chinese."

DAY FOURTEEN

Oct. 4, 1989
K-617 Potemkin
North Pacific Ocean

At the end of his midday watch, McCreary headed to find a cup of whatever these scraggly Russians drank for a pick-me-up. Whitefeather and LaRoy met him near the enlisted men's mess, where a dozen men lounged, eating leftover moose stew and smoking their stinking, hand-rolled cigarettes.

"How much longer until we're in L.A.?" Whitefeather asked.

"Romanenko says we'll be there by nightfall."

"I don't trust that man, Major," Whitefeather said quietly.

"Me, either," McCreary replied. "But he's the only who can steer the boat. You got any way of knowin' whether we're headin' in the right direction?"

Whitefeather closed his eyes. He breathed deeply, then said, "Southeast, bearing one-three-zero degrees. Straight to Hollywood."

Beside him, LaRoy shook his head in admiration.

"But there's somethin' brewin'," Whitefeather said when he opened his eyes. "We been chattin' up the crew. See that chief over yonder?" He pointed at a huge, slouching figure, eating stew from a wooden spoon. It was none other than Big Sasha herself.

LaRoy leaned in. "Your girlfriend's their torpedo man."

"So?"

Whitefeather smiled. "She says they've got five nukes."

McCreary jumped back, startled. "Soviet subs only have conventional torpedoes! Just like ours! The Russians signed away their…" and he trailed off. Another broken Soviet treaty.

At that moment, Romanenko's voice sounded over the intercom, summoning McCreary back to the bridge.

"Should we tell him we know about the nukes?" LaRoy asked as they turned to go.

"Not just yet," McCreary said. "Let's play this close to the vest."

McCreary ordered his men to follow him and, on the way out of the mess, turned and looked at Big Sasha. There she was, glaring at him, shoveling a mouthful of stew into her crooked maw.

Romanenko had put the submarine back on battle stations, the bridge bathed in a menacing red light. Romanenko was in full dress uniform, arms behind his back, standing erect. McCreary paused at the aft entrance and discretely gestured for LaRoy and Whitefeather to remain where they were.

"What can I do for you, Lieutenant?" McCreary asked.

"We are approaching the California coastline," Romanenko said, crisply. "I would like you and your men to remain on the bridge in case we run into any... unexpected welcome from the United States Navy."

McCreary studied Romanenko's Class As. The new uniform didn't make much sense. "You clean up real good," he said. "But why the Sunday best?"

Romanenko looked down and smiled. "This is a special occasion. It's not every day that a Soviet officer surrenders."

Well, get used to it, McCreary almost said.

Romanenko walked to the periscope and summoned McCreary to have a look.

It took a moment for his eyes to adjust. The sun was out, blue sky, purple waves. And floating dead ahead was a hulking, blue-gray shape, grooved and glistening in the sun. Seagulls orbited it, darting in, sailing back up into the blue.

"What is that?" McCreary asked.

"The ultimate reaping of the American war machine," Romanenko said. "A dead blue whale. Half as long as the *Potemkin.* No signs of injury. Radiation killed that beast!"

McCreary felt a heavy hand land on his shoulder. Whitefeather. The big sergeant stooped to look at the lens, and then quickly pulled away. He didn't say anything, but McCreary saw one heartbreaking thing on the Indian's face: a single tear.

McCreary glared at Romanenko. "That's as much your fault as ours! In fact, this whole thing was your side's doin'. The United States never invades a country just because we can!"

Romanenko smirked. "Tell that to your Native American friend."

McCreary fidgeted as Whitefeather lowered a protective hand on his shoulder once more. "Well, that's different!" McCreary said.

"And to the Mexicans. Did they just give your western states away for free?"

"We won that in a war, fair and square!"

"The Philippines!"

"We brought them freedom!"

"Hawaii!"

"We brought them God!"

McCreary and his men monitored the status of the *Potemkin's* reactor. He had spent the past two hours under a cloud, running Romanenko's harsh rhetoric through his fatigued mind. There was no convincing some people.

McCreary's dark reverie was interrupted by a sudden chattering from the crewmen stationed at various positions around the bridge. Warbling tones, bells, and whistles sounded from the cracked equipment. Something dead ahead. Perhaps it was the North American landmass, starting to swing into view.

"Major McCreary," Romanenko said from the periscope. "Something you should see."

McCreary stood. He glanced at Whitefeather, whose eyes had gone cloudy. Something wasn't right. McCreary looked through the periscope's viewfinder.

The first time he'd seen a Megajunk through a periscope, McCreary had thought he'd heard a distant gong; this time, he heard a symphony's worth, a titanic crashing. Surrounding the *Potemkin* was a fleet of Chinese ships, identical to the first. Stunned, McCreary spun the periscope wildly, left, right, left again, and then two frantic circles. Everywhere he looked, nothing but masts and battened, silvery sails, spreading to the horizon.

He pulled his head away, and called for Romanenko... who stood by the entrance to the bridge, one Markov pistol leveled at McCreary's gut, another pointed at Yevgeny, who manned the helm.

"You said we were approaching California!" McCreary cried.

"That's the best part, Major," Romanenko said with a crooked smile. "We *are* approaching California. And so are they." He laughed. "Congratulations, Major McCreary. You have helped me survive a most ill-timed mutiny and to deliver the *Potemkin* to its new owners—the Chinese People's Liberation Navy! Thanks to you, the new standard bearers of the workers' revolution now have a functioning, repairable submarine—along with the last five nuclear weapons on earth."

"Your torpedoes," McCreary heard himself mutter.

"All of you mutinous apes," Romanenko said to the crew, as Whitefeather and LaRoy entered and froze. "When you hanged Captain Aristov and his political officer, you failed to execute the right *zambolit*! For your misplaced loyalty to me, you are to be handed over to the Chinese. You should be ashamed of yourselves. Betraying the Motherland! Betraying the Revolution!"

McCreary looked around at the half-dozen sailors on the bridge, expecting them to rise up and rush Romanenko. Instead, all they did was hang their heads.

"What's all this about?" McCreary asked. But before Romanenko could answer, everything came together on its own: the Megajunk, Romanenko's role in the mutiny, the L.A. Free Zone—and Romanenko's willingness to "help" Lonestar Tactical Unit One.

"My American slang leaves something to be desired, Major," Romanenko said, "but in this glorious war, the Chinese are to be... *the knockout blow.* Their involvement did not end with the seizure of Hawaii."

So the Soviet treachery was even deeper than McCreary had suspected. "The Superbridge," he said. "Tricking General Pearce into moving up to Alaska—"

"—to draw him away from one million Chinese, ready to flood Southern California and march in solidarity with the Soviet Army, all over the once-proud Stars and Stripes. And for our Asian brothers, California shall be their reward!"

"What in the hell do the Chinese want with California?" LaRoy asked. "It's a shit-hole!"

"At ease, Sergeant!" McCreary barked over his shoulder.

"No, no, Major," Romanenko said. "Your enlisted man poses an excellent question. I'm sure you are aware of our Chinese partners and their high birthrate. Overcrowded cities. Famines. Food shortages. Families compelled to have but one child. This led to a... culling of female babies. Now, the Chinese nation is short of women."

And so the second part of the Great Communist Plot Against America fell into place, with an echo in McCreary's mind like the shutting of a giant tomb. Disastrous Communist farming policy had compelled the Soviets to steal the breadbasket of the world; Mao's murderous population control would bring the Chinese to America's golden shore for an even more... precious treasure.

"Your cities of Los Angeles. Hollywood. *Beverly Hills*," Romanenko continued. "Home to millions of beautiful American women."

The thought hurt McCreary's brain. "How many boats?"

"Seventy-two."

"Of those Megajunks? But how could they build so many?"

"I am sorry. My English sometimes is terrible. Seventy-two *hundred*."

Romanenko turned his attention to Yevgeny and pressed the Markov's barrel against his temple. In Russian that McCreary understood all too well, the Soviet officer gave Yevgeny the order to surface.

McCreary emerged from the conning tower, blinking in the sun, with three Chinese sailors in front of him and three behind. A veritable horde of them had swarmed the *Potemkin* belowdecks. McCreary, LaRoy, and especially Whitefeather towered over each of his complement of guards. Still, each diminutive man brandished an AK-47 and marched so smartly it was a wonder they weren't all kicking each other in the behind. Waiting for them on the *Potemkin's* aft deck was a squad of twenty more Chinese Marines, each dressed in battle gray-green, so focused they could have been clones.

The *Potemkin* was a mighty ship, but each of the dozen Megajunks soared, like daunting cliffs of metal and weaponry. The twin catwalks extending from the nearest junk's hull didn't so much as dock with the *Potemkin's* stern as grab it and hold tight.

"Here is where the American dream dies," Romanenko said into his car as they marched toward the nearest catwalk. "The baseball game is in its ninth inning. The apple pie is reduced to crumbs. And Mom? Soon she will be a Chinese concubine."

During the fifteen minutes it took for the *Potemkin* to blow its tanks and surface, the only mystery that remained was why Romanenko hadn't engineered a surrender to the first junk they'd encountered. But now he knew. Romanenko wanted to see McCreary's expression, to enjoy his anguish in the face of overwhelming odds.

They walked across the catwalk into the junk, before a giant silver elevator that could have held a hundred men.

Romanenko, Lonestar Group, and their complement of guards climbed aboard, and a few moments later stood on the ship's expansive bamboo deck.

The ship's masts rose hundreds of feet in the air. Chinese sailors dangled from cables and ropes that draped the deck, hoisting silvery sails, or, high above, making repairs with portable welding kits. Tiny, glowing sparks fell from the air like golden snow.

"Behold," Romanenko said in hushed tones. "Look to the horizon, Major! See that forest of masts! A man could walk from one horizon to another upon these decks and not dip so much as a toe in the Pacific. And did the men who built these glorious machines work for profit? For a percentage? No! They did it for the glory of work itself. The Chinese laborer has something to teach even the most disciplined Russian worker!"

McCreary shook his head, disgusted. He spoke low to the Russian as they were led across the deck toward the superstructure. "You think these fellas are gonna be satisfied with a bunch of bottle-blondes? The average Chinese schoolboy is taught that his homeland stretches into Siberia and points west. Once we're out of the way they'll turn on y'all in a New York minute."

"Then we shall welcome them in the spirit of One World Socialism!"

McCreary snickered. "I don't remember the last Mongolian invasion working out too well for Mother Russia."

A moment later, standing before them was the warrior that McCreary had spotted through the periscope. He was quite a specimen—tanned skin, shining black hair down to his shoulders and a mustache that teased the front of his blue silk robe. He stepped over a length of cable and stood before them, adjusting the curved sword on his hip. The escorts, all two dozen of them, formed a circle around the man and his new guests.

"Admiral Tso Tsung-tang," Romanenko said, clicking his heels. "I present to you the submarine *Potemkin,* her remaining stockpile of five nuclear torpedoes, her mutinous crew—and these three American soldiers." The Soviet bowed.

Tso studied each of the three members of Lonestar with what looked like casual disinterest. He turned to Romanenko.

"Good work, Lieutenant," Tso said in flawless English. "And if I remember correctly, your fee for delivering this … cargo… was quite reasonable."

Romanenko chuckled, self-consciously. "Yes, Admiral. I believe your agents had offered me the Hawaiian island of Ni'ihau—" whereupon Romanenko's severed head bounced across the metal deckplate and struck McCreary's boots.

McCreary jumped back, startled and sickened, into Whitefeather's unyielding frame. Tso sheathed his sword. Romanenko's headless body stood at attention for a moment, spouting blood from its neck in a lazy glut. Then it fell.

Stomach churning, McCreary averted his gaze downward—and was peering back into Romanenko's face. The lieutenant's mouth worked open, closed, open, closed. His blue eyes locked onto McCreary's, radiating confusion, anger, and then nothing.

"Thank you for your service to the Revolution, Lieutenant Romanenko," Tso said with a bemused smile. "But I'm afraid we will be unable to hold up our end of the bargain." He called out an order in Chinese to the men behind McCreary. One of them grabbed Romanenko's severed head by its hair and hurled it overboard. Four more marines grabbed the rest of the lieutenant, one limb each, and similarly tossed it over the side. Finally, five boys in their early teens, dressed as smartly as the others, appeared with mops, buckets, and a large squeegee. Romanenko's neck-fountain had covered the deck in blood, but within ten seconds, the young detachment had erased all evidence of his existence. One even wiped McCreary's boots with a shiny cloth.

Tso's eyes shifted to McCreary. "Ah, and now we have the proud members of Lonestar Tactical Unit One. I am honored to have you with us aboard the *Chairman Mao*."

McCreary didn't answer. Whitefeather kept to his stoic ways. And for once, even LaRoy held his tongue.

Tso smiled. "Come now, Major McCreary. Lieutenant Romanenko met a spy's death. He had outgrown his usefulness to the Joint Communist Command in Moscow. I was merely following orders. Your country is about to lose this war, but you and your comrades have fought honorably. Come! Our Supreme Commander would like to have a word with you."

Tso and his men led them into the superstructure, past a cavernous bridge that was a hive of activity and gleaming, modern computer screens. The hallways were ornately decorated with gold, ivory, and jade. Silk banners fluttered in the air-conditioned breeze. Each had a phrase sewn into it, the Chinese characters winding around each other like red serpents.

Tso and the squad of marines led them to a narrow room. Bootsteps echoed off beige marble floors. Two scantily clad Asian women stood beside an empty throne formed from carved stone dragons. Behind it was a computer display the size of a drive-in movie screen showing a map of the world, continents covered in huge swaths of red: the Soviet Union. China. Australia. Europe. South America.

The Western United States.

Western Canada.

Alaska.

Only the American Midwest and Free Canada remained. That, and a tiny patch of Southern California. The Chinese fleet was represented by a cluster of several thousand red dots in tight formation.

He couldn't help but feel pride that the tattered remnants of the American military had held their part of the country. The front lines stretching from Texas to Montana hadn't budged since McCreary had taken off in the Black Hawk two weeks before. But McCreary's hopes were dashed when he picked out three military symbols. The Tenth Mountain Division still lodged in the Rockies—and two more divisions, both commanded by General Pearce, blinking at the Canadian border. Heading off to fight an imaginary Russian foe in Alaska while the real threat lay off Catalina Island.

And all of it was McCreary's fault.

"Like me," Admiral Tso said in hushed tones, "Generalissimo Li Chiang studied in the United States. His command of English and… American culture… is even better than my own. As you shall see."

Just then, Generalissimo Li emerged from behind a towering silk curtain. He was dressed not in Tso's flowing Ming Dynasty robes, nor in the standard-issue People's Republic green-and-red. No, Li Chiang presented himself to the men of Lonestar Tactical Unit One in gray wool. Shiny black riding boots. Jangling spurs. A crisp gray cowboy hat, emblazoned with a star. Holding up his trousers was a silver buckle, with the capital letters "CS", framed on each side with… the Confederate Stars and Bars.

It was becoming too much.

McCreary sighed, "You must be General…"

"Li!" the general drawled happily. "General Li!"

"Uh-boy," Whitefeather breathed.

The general, all five-foot-two of him, stepped down the dais, stopping a few feet from McCreary and his men. He pulled out wood-handled pistols—each an impeccable replica of a 1851 Colt Navy, McCreary noted with some amazement—and happily waved them in the air, without a hint of menace. He shoved them back in his holsters, and smiled. "So happy to see a real American—what do you think?" he asked in perfectly unaccented English.

"A mighty fine likeness," McCreary deadpanned. "Fellas?"

"Grow ya' a silver beard, and you'll look just like him," LaRoy said.

"Spittin' image," Whitefeather said. Whereupon the big Indian turned his head—and spat.

If General Li noticed Whitefeather's show of disrespect, he didn't let on. He walked to McCreary and examined him, looking up more than a foot into his face. "Your accent: Texas? East Texas? Fifty miles west of Texarkana?"

"Close enough," McCreary said. "Sergeant Whitefeather here's from Oklahoma, and Sergeant LaRoy's a son of West Virginia."

Li beamed at all three of them. "Three sons of the Confederacy! So happy to have y'all on board!" He stuck out his hand. "Li Chiang, hailin' from Tianjin, matriculated in military and computer science, University of Georgia,

Class a' '72! And as you can see, I've returned to see that the South shall rise again!"

And when McCreary shook his hand, General Li held his hat to his head and let loose a Rebel yell that would have pleased Stonewall Jackson himself.

Li smiled into McCreary's eyes. When neither McCreary nor his men smiled in return, he searched their faces with growing confusion. "But… but… Texas! Oklahoma! Virginia!"

"West Virginia, actually, sir," LaRoy said. "See, we split off from Virginia to stay with the Union. My great-great granddaddy commanded the 325th West Virginia Militia at the Siege of Petersburg. So I ain't no secessionist, no sir."

"Oklahoma was Indian Territory during the War Between the States," Whitefeather said next. "And I don't take kindly to the idea of my African brothers bein' led around in chains."

That left McCreary. Li's silent plea for approval fell on the major.

"Sorry, General," he said, "I just want to go home."

Li turned, arms suddenly behind his back. He stomped back to his throne and sat, an angry dwarf, cowboy hat pushed forward across his brow. Shooting forward, he strode down the steps in front of his throne and swept his arm toward the giant world map. "Do you see this? This! This entire planet! It's ours!"

"Almost," McCreary said. "But not quite. Looks like you forgot parts of Canada there. And the Eastern U.S.— including your precious South. Other than Florida, they don't seem to be too keen to go Commie just yet."

"Just wait." Li shot back. "Soon, we shall turn the entire United States into *our* plantation." He barked in Chinese at a man standing at a computer terminal. Slowly, the map transformed. "Witness the People's Fleet landing in Los Angeles! Once your unified command crosses safely into Canada, by sunset tomorrow!" On the giant map, the red dots moved ashore and turned the Los Angeles Free Zone to instant crimson.

"Texas!" Li cried. "Louisiana! Flowing north and east from Mississippi! Alabama! Tennessee!" He glowered triumphantly at McCreary as the remainder of the United States, indeed the world, glowed the color of blood.

"A fancy simulation, General," McCreary said. "You still gotta do the real thing. And unless you got wheels on these boats, there's still a lot of fightin' to do."

Faster than Tso with his sword, Li drew both pistols. McCreary expected a bullet between the eyes. Instead, the diminutive general spun and fired both pistols at the girls standing beside his throne. Each had worn an over the shoulder sarong; with deadly accuracy, Li fired a bullet through the clasps holding up the robes. In a flash of smoke and tiny sparks, the sarongs fell. Both girls shrieked and held the robes to their slender chests, scrambling behind the curtain in shame.

Li holstered his .45s. "I am not a man to trifle with," he sneered, "as you shall soon discover."

The golden sun set behind the towering masts of the Peoples' Fleet. McCreary found himself standing at one end of the *Chairman Mao*'s aft deck, holding a pair of loaded Colt .45s at his side. LaRoy and Whitefeather stood to his right, unarmed. At least a hundred Chinese marines, each with bayonet-fixed AK-47, lined the deck on either side. And at the other end of this human alley, standing at the base of the foremast, stood General Li.

Blindfolded, hat off, holster belt at his feet, a single pistol held limply at his side.

"You will never get a better chance, McCreary!" Li called. "I am blind, and I possess but a single bullet! I promise, I won't shoot until you do!"

"What the hell's he doing?" LaRoy asked.

"With the Chinese it's always psychological," Whitefeather said. "He's playin' with you, Major."

McCreary stood in silence. This was impossible. He was a fair shot with a pistol, to be sure, but Li was a good hundred feet away. That breeze was pretty strong…

"Major," Whitefeather said, "there's an easy solution here…"

And even if he managed to hit Li between the eyes—and McCreary gave himself even odds at best—there was the unpleasant matter of a horde of Chinese AK-47s…

"Major," Whitefeather said, "you gotta listen to me…"

And that didn't even count Admiral Tso and his magic sword. Lord knew what that guy was capable of…

Faintly at first, but growing in intensity, General Li's chuckle grew into a full-throated laugh.

"Major!"

"What?!?"

"SHOOT HIM!"

"Okay."

McCreary raised his pistol, and without any conscious thought, pulled the trigger.

To the major's great surprise, the top of General Li's head disappeared.

Chaos ensued.

He hit the deck and came up firing. McCreary was dimly aware of Whitefeather grabbing the Chinese marine to his right and twisting his head almost off his body. The tiny man fell hard, but not before Whitefeather snatched his AK and sprayed Chinese lead. McCreary didn't actually see what magic LaRoy performed, but the West Virginian had found his own assault rifle and joined the party.

Lonestar Group, armed once more, fell into the kind of lethal teamwork that reminded McCreary of a watch. A Swiss watch. A Swiss watch of death.

With Whitefeather and LaRoy armed for medium range, McCreary aimed for the closest targets. He picked off four, then five, then six marines, before they even got off a shot. The bulk of their comrades, caught by surprise, fumbled with their weapons, mistakenly shot their own men, or dove ineffectively for cover behind machinery, winches, and piles of sails.

"Back to the sub!" McCreary ordered. "I'll cover you! And if I don't make it, you've got to get to L.A.!"

There was no time to argue. Whitefeather and LaRoy disappeared through the superstructure's main hatch, blasting away, cutting a path of death in front of them.

McCreary turned and fired his last remaining rounds into five charging Chinese troops. Each fell in a twisted, collective grimace of death. He reached down to pick up a discarded AK-47 when he felt cold steel against his neck. McCreary froze.

"You have fought well, Major," Admiral Tso said. "More importantly, you have rid me of the unseemly, politically appointed, and quite insane General Li. The Chinese war effort thanks you."

"Just an American boy doing what I can," McCreary said. He stood and raised both hands behind his head.

The sword lifted from his neck; McCreary resisted the urge to believe that the good admiral was giving him a reprieve. He fell to his knees and grabbed the rifle, feeling the faint flicker of steel across the back of his head. He was aware of maddening detail—a blizzard of his own greasy black hairs falling around him; a glimpse of the admiral's feet in bamboo sandals, poking from under the hem of his robes; the slick, cold metal of the AK slipping into his hand with the help of the Almighty himself.

Rolling onto his back, McCreary raised the weapon with the intention of shooting. Instead, he saw sparks as Tso knocked the barrel aside with his sword. McCreary squeezed and kept the Kalashnikov from spinning over the railing. He rolled as Tso's sword came down right where his head had been a fraction of a second before.

McCreary got to his feet and raised the rifle again. Tso had his sword raised, a perfect shot into the admiral's chest. But the sword flashed down before McCreary could squeeze the trigger. There was a faint tug, and the weapon's banana clip spun to the deck. McCreary squeezed the trigger anyway, the remaining bullet clanging off the sword's edge, perfectly deflected.

Tso waved his sword hypnotically, like the head of a cobra. "Your rifle is spent," Tso chuckled. "I have brought you into the world of blades, and in our equality we are vastly unequal."

McCreary gritted his teeth and thrust forward with the bayonet in five quick jabs. Tso laughed, parrying each. McCreary was too fatigued to feel intimidation. His bayonet training took over: long afternoons at Lackland Air Force Base under the Texas sun, being screamed at by Army pukes in Smokey Bear hats. Stabbing tires. Stabbing trees, stabbing under live fire, slashing until it became a part of his body.

As he parried and thrust with the AK-47, McCreary spied his only hope. Tso was stepping backward blindly toward the railing of the ship's squarish bow. If he could pin the admiral to the rails, maybe he had a chance.

But a few yards short, a pair of hatches behind Tso sprang open. A half-dozen Chinese warriors clad in gleaming armor climbed out. Each warrior carried a titanium spear twice as tall as his body. The spearpoints crackled with snaking blue lightning. With three warriors on each side of him, Tso lowered his sword, and laughed. He gave an order, and the spear points dropped toward McCreary in deadly unison.

"That'll be enough for me," McCreary said. He turned and sprinted toward the bridge, dropping the now-useless AK to the deck.

McCreary turned, half expecting to see a fresh platoon of Chinese marines rushing toward him. Instead, the deck was deserted, except for the dead. The boat was alive, though, with the sound of alarms and distant shouts. There was a faint whooshing sound, and a cloud of silvery spray rose over the starboard railing.

Potemkin!

McCreary picked up a fresh rifle from the deck and rushed toward the railing. Sure enough, seventy feet below and a hundred feet ahead, the *Potemkin* was covered in bodies, clad in either white or green. And she was going down. No one from the surrounding ships had fired upon her yet, but McCreary saw and heard guns swinging about.

"Your friends are deserting you, Major!" Tso said behind him. "It is time to give up!"

"Onward, Whitefeather!" McCreary called instead, as the *Potemkin* sank into a cloud of green bubbles. "Onward, Billy LaRoy! Onward, comrades! I wish I could join you!"

No! Enough of that talk!

For the answer was in his right hand.

McCreary stepped onto the railing. As he had a lifetime ago above a high Colorado ravine, he jumped.

McCreary had rarely heard any Asian languages spoken before or during the war, but now he knew how the Chinese swore. Tso's cursing and frantic orders descended upon McCreary as he sailed toward the sub. Two electric spears whizzed past him; they struck the *Potemkin*'s conning tower in a shower of sparks. The cable he'd grabbed—made of pure silk—slung off to the right toward the submerging deck. It was a smooth ride between the two towering hulls, and would have been great fun had the goal been to take a splash in a swimming hole back home. But it wasn't. The target was a submerging island made from steel plate and factory labor—the *Potemkin!* And McCreary was swinging toward it at thirty miles an hour. His boots clanged off the aft deck and the impact tore him away from the cable. He rolled on the deck just as the first AK-47 rounds from above sparked the deck around him.

Bullets flew around his feet, missing him by bare millimeters. Another spear clanged off the deck next to his foot and sailed into the frothy water. If only McCreary could make it to the hatch before one of them cut him in two, or before the entire submarine submerged and drowned him in the chilly waters off Los Angeles.

But of course McCreary made it.

He always made it.

* * *

K-617 Potemkin
Off the Southern California coast

The *Potemkin* settled at the bottom atop a shoal, miraculously invisible from the Chinese junks and smaller patrol craft that circled overhead. There were no depth charges. The Chinese crews had failed to remove the ship's five nuclear torpedoes, and they wanted their precious cargo intact.

The Russians had surprised and overpowered all of the Chinese who had boarded the *Potemkin,* killing each in bloody, hand-to-hand combat, and in the process had lost more than a dozen of their own. Yevgeny had but nine comrades left, including Big Sasha. Worse, the fight had destroyed the ship's fire control system. The crew doubted they could fire the torpedoes.

Now, the survivors huddled on the shattered, dimly lit bridge. "There's only one thing to do," McCreary said. "We sneak out of here and surface out of sight of the Chinese. You men get off the boat. Make it to L.A. I'll steer back under the fleet and set off the nukes."

"You'll never make it past the blockade," Whitefeather said.

"Then I'll detonate early," McCreary said. "Takin' out half the fleet's better than leavin' all of 'em."

"It's still a losing fight once they come ashore," LaRoy said quietly.

"Then we fight harder!" McCreary said. "If they want our country and our women, dammit, make 'em bleed for it!"

But LaRoy stared down at the deck. For the first time, the energetic West Virginian sounded like he was running down.

"He is right, *Amerikanskiy,*" Yevgeny said. "It is time to quit. The Asians are too strong! We shall sail toward Los

Angeles. Scuttle *Potemkin* to keep it from the Chinese dogs. We go ashore and have glorious party with your American girls until Chinese arrive. We drink! We dance!"

"I don't quit!" McCreary said. "*America* doesn't quit!"

Yevgeny stepped forward. "You are finding out what we Russians have known since birth! Communism never pretty! Is never smart! But is strong! Perhaps with America's resources, the Revolution will do what Karl Marx intended—share wealth, feed poor, bring equality to all. America was great! But that long ago!"

"*NO!*" McCreary roared.

Around him, the crew—Russians and Americans—froze.

"Russians invade countries to bring Communism!" McCreary testified. "We *liberate* them—to bring freedom! Communists revere dead men with strange ideas—Lenin! Stalin! Marx! Not us! We worship the glory of George Washington—and Jesus Christ! And while you Communists have a corrupt politburo ruled by one political party... we have a Congress—ruled by *two* political parties!

"You Russians, and your allegiance to... *the group*," he went on, disgusted, gathering strength like a Kansas thunderstorm. "Not us—when Americans want to get things done, we join *teams*! Like this one!"

Slowly, the Russians nodded.

"And ain't no one gonna come ashore and cart off our pretty girls!" McCreary said. He pointed at his men: "LaRoy, Whitefeather: That's your job!"

Both men smiled wearily.

Yevgeny's friendly, crooked yellow-toothed grin returned. "Once again," he said, "I underestimate your resolve, *Amerikanskiy*. What can we do to help?"

161

*   *   *

The sailors steered the limping *Potemkin* due north, surfacing in safe, calm waters. The Chinese fleet lay far to the south. The entire crew clambered to the deck, readying the sub's launches for the treacherous break toward shore. McCreary lay his hand on LaRoy's shoulder: "You and Whitefeather have to make it back. If I can take care of the Chinese, our boys have a fightin' chance."

"Always tryin' to play the hero, sir," LaRoy said. With tears in his eyes, he hugged McCreary fiercely.

Whitefeather pushed past them, loading weapons and provisions into the launches. McCreary knew that Whitefeather refused to ever say goodbye.

McCreary felt a heavy hand land on his shoulder. He turned, and found himself looking up into the carved granite face of Big Sasha. She spoke in Russian.

"She needs to stay with you," Yevgeny translated.

McCreary shook his head. "You said the torpedoes can be activated from the bridge."

More baritone commands, gestures and explanation from the towering she-Russian: "She says too much can go wrong. Big Sasha has no love for Chinese. She lost all brothers in border skirmish of '67. She says it is wrong for you to do alone."

There was no time to argue. McCreary stood at attention and offered his hand. Sasha gave McCreary a crisp salute.

Yevgeny and Sasha guided McCreary down to the com station. Sasha already had ventured to the forward torpedo bay. After a crash course in holding the sub on a steady tack, Yevgeny shook McCreary's hand and clapped his shoulder. For Yevgeny, the war was over and he didn't care how it ended, as long as he left alive. It was the Russian way.

McCreary felt his throat tighten. He didn't turn to bid his men farewell. It wasn't time for sentimentality. It was time to save the Free World.

DAY FIFTEEN

Oct. 5, 1989
K-617 Potemkin

The Soviet sub was silent. Army Major Mike McCreary stood next to the submerged sub's com station, scanning dials he barely understood, praying he was reading them right and keeping the sub on a steady course.

After Whitefeather, LaRoy, and the Russian crew had departed, McCreary expected everything to go wrong. The submarine's engines would blow, or its reactor would fail. But it didn't.

Just after midnight, with thirty minutes remaining until detonation, McCreary switched the periscope to infrared. As he frantically scanned ahead for any sign of the masts, one horrible thought, always nagging him at the periphery of his mind, became set in concrete:

They would never get close enough to the Chinese to do any damage. He'd calculated twelve megatons on board. It would make a lot of noise. Perhaps a halfway decent blast wave. But if the Chinese pickets got to him before Sasha pushed the button down, it wouldn't sink the entire fleet.

For a moment, McCreary thought he saw a lone ship. Perhaps another sub. Certainly Chinese. A low, hulking shape, big enough for waves to break against its hull. As the *Potemkin* steamed closer, its true form revealed itself. McCreary shook his head.

You again.

The *Potemkin* sailed past the dead whale, onward in its suicidal quest.

McCreary's problem remained. He needed to find the Chinese fleet. Surface inside it, dead center. Bathe it in nuclear fire. Save the world.

But there was no way.

Or was there?

McCreary sprinted away from the com station and toward the torpedo room. There, Sasha strolled calmly among the horizontal green tubes that lined the walls. She came to an open break, where one of the five sleek black torpedoes lay nestled in their cradles of death. Their nose cones were open, and within each, McCreary could see the synchronized timers ticking down to doomsday.

02:13:27... 02:13:26... 02:13:25...

McCreary caught the torpedowoman's attention. She jerked upright. Glared at him.

Crazy American. What now?

He pointed to one of the torpedoes, and held up both hands, all ten fingers.

Wait.

With no apparent knowledge of English, it took Sasha several minutes to understand McCreary's scheme. And even when she did understand it, she laughed deeply. She lowered her hand onto McCreary's shoulder and shook her head, until a new fit of laughter rose and she backed away, holding her gut.

"You got a better idea?" he asked.

But the old girl just laughed and laughed.

The new plan was underway. Without the use of its periscope, the *Potemkin* resumed its course. And wouldn't you know it, the remaining sonar capability flickered back to life, and McCreary picked up the Chinese fleet once more. The vast sea of blips had moved closer to shore, but if the Chinese fell for the ruse, and the sub could penetrate the fleet unmolested, they stood half a chance.

McCreary thought about laying flat on his back on the gently thrumming deck. He could remain here, listening to the timers, and meet his end. Did he want to live in an America wracked by war? What kind of place would it be, even if good prevailed? Bombed-out cities. Food riots. Radioactive death zones. Why, if the wind wasn't blowing just right, twelve megatons going off at sea this close to Southern California wasn't going to be good for the old food chain.

But...

Sunny.

His wife might still be alive. Was the hypnotic mumbo-jumbo still in control of her pretty little head, or did that hocus-pocus have a shelf life? Just now, she could be waking up in a field somewhere, scared, wondering what had happened. More importantly, wondering where he was. He'd have a story or two to tell her! He might have to leave a few parts out.

But it wasn't to be. He and Big Sasha had chosen death, for the benefit of many. His country's last hope:

the warrior's destiny. Perhaps, with the Lord's grace, it would be the last time.

McCreary turned back toward the control room, and walked right into the path of a swinging wrench.

Through a cloud of pain and confusion, McCreary was aware of being picked up and carried. He felt light, as though the arms supporting him could carry the Rock of Gibraltar itself. He blinked and looked up.

Big Sasha!

More Communist treachery!

Why was there always one spy left? Why hadn't he just ordered her to set the timers and leave with the others?

As she walked him heavily through the control room, McCreary fought to get out of her embrace. She merely raised him higher, encircling her arms around him like a bulldozer. It was no use; the blow had temporary crippled him, anyway. He had the strength of a ragdoll. McCreary studied her face in the green glow of the overhead lamps as she clumped heavily through corridors and over bulkheads.

"Hey, Sasha," he rambled weakly. "Take me back to the control room, huh? We gotta stop the Chinese..."

If she understood English, she didn't let on. Within moments, she had brought him to the forward torpedo room. She turned, and lowered him down.

Through his warped vision in the torpedo room's dim light, McCreary had the impression of being lowered into a coffin. It was a sixth torpedo he hadn't noticed before. His back lay on something soft, and he gazed up helplessly into the shadow of Big Sasha's backlit face. Sasha fitted something clear and rubbery over his own. A cool hiss filled the world. McCreary tasted the acrid aroma of pure oxygen.

His mind raced back to his brief foray into Special Forces, where his Navy counterparts boasted of their special torpedoes that could send a man fifty miles to a beach, riding a cloud of bubbles. Apparently, the Spetsnaz boys had the same toys.

But he couldn't entrust America's survival to this man-sized woman. McCreary tried to raise his arms. Sasha answered with a heavy hand to the middle of his chest.

"*Udacha*, Yankee," she said, as sweetly as she could in her rich baritone. And then, in decent English: "You made me feel like woman. For one moment, eh? And for that... I steer boat. Only room in *Spetsnaz* capsule for one!" She leaned down, put a meaty kiss on his forehead. "God bless America!" she said, smiling through crooked teeth, and lowered the torpedo's hatch.

All McCreary could sense after that was a faint red glow. Whether it was some worklight in the torpedo, or his own brain giving way to the abuse it had withstood, he never knew.

There came a surge of acceleration.

A deafening roar.

Standing proudly atop the *Chairman Mao*'s foredeck, facing the rising sun, Admiral Tso Tsung-tang gave the final order: unfurl thousands of sails and set course for Los Angeles. At long last, the bureaucrats back home had stopped wringing their spotted hands.

Since the beginning of the Russians' war, Americans' surprising resistance to the bumbling invasion had frightened the Eight Elders of the Politburo in Beijing. They would leave nothing to chance. They would face no surprises. No resistance from misguided American patriots. *Patience*, the Old Guard had told Tso, as they built in redundancy after redundancy. The invasion fleet had steamed east toward Hawaii Province for provisions, then toward California. More ships. More men. Led by the certifiably insane General Li.

Now, Li was dead. With the American coastline over the horizon, Tso strode along the flagship's railing, arms behind him, robes flapping in the breeze. He turned and tried to take comfort in the mighty expanse of sails and ships that stretched westward behind the *Chairman Mao*, seemingly back to the Taiwan shipyards from whence they'd come.

But the junks gave Tso no comfort. Too much might still go wrong. Just in the past few hours, so much had.

The mutinous *Potemkin.*

The failure to capture her—and her nuclear torpedoes.

And one Major Michael McCreary, the most misguided patriot Tso had ever encountered, who had escaped certain death like the pirate he was. How had such a thing been possible? Were the capitalist dogs correct? Was there, in fact, one Almighty God that controlled the universe?

And worst of all… *was He an American?*

Enough of this fatalistic talk! Soon, Tso would wade ashore, leading an army of one million worker-warriors. They would strike into America's soft, smooth hindquarters.

The thought of cowering, shrieking American starlets brought a smile beneath Tso's flowing mustache.

Behind him, from somewhere else on the *Mao,* or from one of the flanking ships… a cry of alarm!

All up and down the nearby ships, sailors ran to the railings and pointed at the surface of the water. An entire platoon of the *Zhu De*'s marines had abandoned their weapons and stared at the waves below their stations.

More annoyed than alarmed, Tso sprinted to that side of the *Chairman Mao*.

Something enormous had worked its way between the two ships.

Tso felt terror, shame, and the withering gaze of his ancestors. Surely they studied him with disdain from the Celestial Kingdom. This fleet! Its incompetence! How had an enemy somehow...

Tso then realized what the other men had known all along. The beast in the water was flesh, not steel. A once mighty whale. From the decks of the *Zhu De*, Tso heard cheers and laughter and good tidings.

Of all things, a whale!

The ultimate sign of good fortune to a Chinese sailor!

Tso stood straight and adjusted the sword in his sash. He was about to slip back into his conqueror's reverie when something caught his eye. Something swam beneath the beast. Something monstrous.

Gray.

Metal.

Tso realized the truth a millisecond before the world turned white.

Sometime after feeling the torpedo run out of power, and its motor spun down to nothing, McCreary became aware of a thump from either side of the hull. The lid above his head popped open, and he was hit in the face with an unending splash of light and cold, saltwater spray.

McCreary sat up against a painful haze and found himself bobbing in the ocean. The torpedo craft had deployed a set of gray, inflatable wings that barely kept it upright. The waves were half the height of the breakers he'd seen on deck earlier. There was no sign of the sub, no

171

sign of land, and certainly nothing to suggest the Chinese fleet.

But no: there it was, far to the south. A long line of bristling antennas. A hint of sails. A gargantuan forest of them. How far away was the fleet? After washing out of para-rescue school, McCreary had undergone a course in Soviet nukes in order to save his commission and serve his country in a missile silo. Now, sitting helplessly in the ocean, he struggled to remember how much distance he would need to survive.

Twelve megatons. That's third degree burns in a fifteen-mile radius. Certain death from radiation in about as much distance. A blast wave—the hand of God... how far?

He didn't know.

And as it had for Admiral Tso, all color drained from the world but one.

McCreary felt instant heat on his face. His eyes closed, but he saw right through his eyelids, then through the arm that he raised to shield himself. The light was God's flashbulb. He was aware of his ulna's outline.

Pure X-rays! he thought. Straight through to my brain!

The glare faded. McCreary lifted his head from the crook of his arm. The sky had returned to its natural, hazy blue. The torpedo and the waves around it, though, cast twin shadows forward, one set from the sun, and the other from the nuclear hell that the submarine had unleashed.

He craned his neck to take it all in. It loomed above him. The mushroom cloud was an unholy white, the ghost of its immense fireball still churning within it, fading, boiling, refusing to die. McCreary wanted to rise up, to lean forward on his knees, to pray to what he had created, to beg forgiveness for the destruction he had

172

unleashed. It was then that the rumbling started, arising as if from the sea itself.

All along the horizon, McCreary saw an approaching wall of white. Spreading. Fast. Rising. The world washed away again!

Huntington Beach, California
17:30

McCreary lifted his head from the sand and looked around. He heard music. Jangling rhythms. Someone singing about everyone having an ocean. His eyes swam into focus. All around him he heard the sound of crashing waves. A tinny transistor radio. The sound of women laughing. The sun was low.

He was dead. This was heaven. Women walking around with next to nothing on. The smell of barbecue and woodsmoke.

He turned his head and saw the Potemkin's launch flipped over on the sand. He got to his knees.

Whitefeather, his shirt off, sat in a beach chair, two women oiling his broad shoulders.

LaRoy sat not far away, holding a beer in each hand. Also shirtless. Lobster red. His smile was one of oblivion. And what was that white stuff on his nose? Where had he gotten the sunglasses? LaRoy spotted McCreary and smiled. Instead of rushing over, however, the West Virginian, raised one bottle in salute.

McCreary stood, body weak, feeling a bad burn on the back of his neck and hoping that it was from the sun.

The beach was crowded. An unending party of beautiful girls and muscular men. A huge group of

173

them had gathered around the Russian sailors. Beer flowed. Surfboards poked up from the sand, a mockery of the tombstones that would someday line every mile of American road when the war was done. But instead of the smoke of burning cities, all McCreary could smell was the smoke from a dozen campfires.

McCreary staggered to LaRoy. "What happened here, Sergeant?" he asked. His mouth tasted funny. Metallic. God knew how much radiation—

"Your boy's had too many brewskis, bro," said a teenage kid, padding toward him. "You got any money? That guy owes me ten bucks for the beer he drank!"

"You owe him much more than that," McCreary muttered. "Sergeant! Did you alert General Pearce?"

LaRoy smiled, intoxicated. "Oh yes, sir!" he said. "Yevgeny over there helped me rig a shortwave. We caught the general before he was crossin' into Canada. By now, I imagine they've turned back into Montana and they're ready to give an ass whuppin to what's left of Ivan!" At that, LaRoy dropped one of his beers into the sand, gave a wobbly salute, and passed out.

The Californian kid sidled up to McCreary, uncomfortably close, the stench of marijuana coming through his grimy pores. "He said you guys were on a Russian submarine," the kid said. "Was that what blew up? Way out in the ocean! It looked like a mushroom cloud. Like I've seen in the movies!"

McCreary ignored him, but here came two other kids, one a boy, one a girl. The girl was hanging out of her orange bikini. McCreary wanted to tell her to put something on, but the view was tremendous. The kid with her had a big mop of curly blond hair. He glared at McCreary like a poodle staring down a wolf. Poodle-boy didn't like some old guy in a filthy uniform staring at his girl. Too bad.

"Hey, man, are you guys soldiers?" Poodle-boy asked. "I don't want any baby-killer types messin' up my beach."

McCreary felt the sand trickling out of his hair. He reached up and brushed at it furiously. "Don't you kids know there's a war on?" he asked.

The first kid laughed. "There's always a war on somewhere, man," he said.

Such ignorance. Impossible! "The Russian army—!" McCreary began. He pointed over his shoulder. "The Chinese! Big fleet! Invasion!"

The long-haired kid cut him off: "You're too uptight, man. Here: smoke this." He tried to hand McCreary a marijuana cigarette.

McCreary stared at it, disbelieving, and knocked it out of the kid's hand.

"Hey, man!" the kid whined angrily.

McCreary was already moving up the beach. Whitefeather snored, the most well-deserved nap in the history of modern warfare. McCreary reached between the women, touched the sergeant's head, and moved on.

That left the Russians. They would know. They always knew. "Yevgeny!" McCreary yelled. "What the hell happened?"

"The blast wave!" the Russian chief called back. "It knocked you out of the *Spetsnaz* capsule! I found you bobbing in the water. I saved you from drowning! Russian strength always prevails, *Amerikanskiy*! Now you owe me your life!" At Yevgeny's feet, an adoring throng of half-naked girls sat. One of them produced what looked like a kerosene lamp. She flicked a disposable Bic lighter at a valve in front of it and stuck her mouth into the top, breathing deep.

At that, Major Michael J. McCreary, United States Army, shook his head. He fished the Medal of Honor out of his pocket, rubbed its tarnished surface with his thumb, and put it back, safe. He pulled a discarded AK-47 out of the sand. Dusted it off. Slung it over his shoulder. The warrior never found love for his labors, even when the people he was saving didn't know or care.

McCreary cast one more look over his shoulder at the party on the beach. Russian sailors danced with American girls.

Fifty yards ahead, the partiers had parked a row of cars—convertibles, VW Bugs, and an honest-to-goodness wood-paneled station wagon. Somewhere in that wide, beautiful, messed-up country, his wife waited. He would let his men rest, recon the beach, circle back, and get his outfit back to work. There would be new enemies to defeat, and new freedoms to be won.

And misunderstood or not, the American fighting man couldn't stop the fight until the fight was done.

THE END

AFTERWORD

When Johnny Shaw asked me to contribute to the premiere issue of *Blood & Tacos* back in 2012, I couldn't refuse. It beat paying the money I owed him for used hot tub parts. Johnny, a huge fan of the men's adventure books of the 1970s and '80s, was feeling nostalgic for the old days and wanted to revive the spirit of those old "masterpieces." He began asking the writers he knew to hunt down and "refurbish" whatever rare examples of men's adventure stories they could find.

As luck would have it, I'd been browsing through a swap meet in Coos Bay, Oregon, just the week before. In a shoebox filled with survivalist training manuals, Laser Tag accessories, and tarnished throwing stars, I discovered a tattered copy of *Battleground U.S.S.A.: Texasgrad.* The author was a mysterious figure from Skokie, Indiana, named Max Auger. In the acknowledgments Auger thanked his parents for letting him live in their basement despite recently turning "two-score-and-two." From what I could tell offhand, the 1984 novel was about the invasion of the United States, executed by an unholy alliance of the Soviet Union, "Communist China," and the combined land and air forces of *El Ejército Mexicano.* Amused, I paid a quarter for it and went on my way.

Turns out it was money well spent. *Texasgrad* was a perfect example of how the men's adventure genre had "evolved" in the 1980s. Thank you, Mr. Reagan. Even if I'd wanted to read the whole thing, the copy I found was completely trashed. More than half of its 180 pages were gone. Much of what remained was stained with God-knew-what.

Fortunately, there was enough left between *Texasgrad's* frayed and soiled covers for me to boil it down to a short story. I enjoyed getting to know *Texasgrad's* characters— Captain Mike McCreary, his wife, Sunny, specialists Charles Whitefeather and Billy LaRoy, et al. And *Blood & Tacos* went on to do surprisingly well. Johnny put out four issues, each packed with stories just like *Texasgrad*. Some of these even came out on podcast, mine included.

Last summer Johnny put out the call for *Blood & Tacos* sequels, and fortune struck again. I'd taken another job, in New England. The day before Johnny tracked me down and called me up in his typical drunken stupor, my wife had dragged me to a quaint Yankee antique store. Lying in a 10¢ box was No. 2 in the Battleground U.S.S.A. series. A dime paid out fair and square, *Red Dusk* came home.

I did a bit more research this time but learned nothing new about Auger. Yet I did uncover a few things about *Red Dusk* itself, which almost took down an entire New York publishing house. Someone at the company in question had read *Texasgrad* and decided that he had discovered the next Tom Clancy. The same editor also liked cocaine. The two facts may or may not be interrelated. The publisher found Auger and gave him $25,000 for a sequel without seeing so much as a new manuscript page. The fight to free America from the Communist horde would resume.

Fueled by dreams that only twenty-five grand can buy, Auger sat down, perhaps at his mother's kitchen table, and feverishly churned out his magnum opus. Sadly, history kept the novel from wide release. As the Cold War looked like it was entering a Reagan Renaissance, *glasnost* and *Perestroika* reared their ugly heads and kicked over the Berlin Wall. American genre readers abruptly lost the Communists they favored as villains. Auger's book has a 1989 copyright. Alas, so does a unified Berlin.

As a bestseller, *Red Dusk* just wasn't going to pan out, and it was too late to cancel the check. Five thousand paperback copies hit the shelves of truck stops everywhere, the hardcover pulped, the dream remaindered. And that, friends, is where the Max Auger trail goes cold once again.

I just hope he used the money to get his own place. Or at least his own room.

ACKNOWLEDGMENTS

I thank the usual suspects: Johnny Shaw, author of *Dove Season, Big Maria,* and *Plaster City,* for helping me interpret Auger's purple prose; our comrade-in-arms Michael Batty, who writes as Bart Lessard (*Rakehell, Full of Days, Dead Men's Teeth*) and who did his usual masterful job as editor and production designer; my beautiful wife, Deidre, who reconstructed the faded, tattered *Red Dusk* cover in her studio; my son, Christopher, who was a fierce stand-in and model for Major Mike McCreary on the redone cover; and, of course, Mr. Brace Godfrey.

Whatever I wrote here is dedicated to my grandparents, Maurice and Lori Benson.

Christopher Blair
Gorham, New Hampshire